"The rumor flyi tried to blackmail Viane. I know you're a little crazy." Arielle winked. "But not that nuts."

"Actually, I did."

Arielle's eyebrows shot up. "Seriously?"

"Seriously. I hoped if I could get hush money from her it would be tantamount to an admission of guilt, something I could take to the gendarmes."

"That's brilliant. So, now the whole town thinks you pushed her down the stairs because she refused to pay you."

"They're wrong. I didn't push her. I kicked her."

"Brittany Ann Thornton, where are your manners?"

Britt allowed herself a small smirk of satisfaction. "It's okay. She pushed me first. After she drugged me with heroin and hit me with a ginormous frying pan. Then she was going to finish me off with a syringe full of nicotine."

Murder Undetected

by

Roxanne Dunn

Murder Undetected

Cover Art by *Kim Mendoza*

The Wild Rose Press, Inc.
PO Box 708
Adams Basin, NY 14410-0708
Visit us at www.thewildrosepress.com

Publishing History
First Edition, 2021
Trade Paperback ISBN 978-1-5092-3868-2
Digital ISBN 978-1-5092-3869-9

Published in the United States of America

Dedication

To my family and friends, near and far, with a heaping bushel of love and gratitude.

Chapter One

Near Seattle

The interview room was empty except for two battered metal chairs on either side of a small, rectangular table bolted to the concrete floor. The only window, high on the wall, had bars on it. The air smelled of institutional disinfectant.

Britt Thornton, candidate for Ph.D. in psychology, buttoned her navy jacket over her anonymous white blouse, like a shield.

Tall, lanky, and dark-haired, seventeen-year-old Tom Watson stepped into the room, then stopped. An expression of disgust flashed across his features. Then anger. In an instant, he replaced it with a smirk.

"Hey, pretty lady." He sauntered toward the table. "You look a lot better than that clown they sent yesterday." He ruffled up his hair and pulled his mouth and eyes into an amazing likeness of Oscar Plitman. "Looked like a mad scientist."

If Oscar, her mentor, had been here yesterday, why had he sent her today?

Focus. Britt sucked in a breath. "Hello, Tom. Please sit down."

"Tom?" With a grin, he looked over his shoulder at the guard, who had closed the door and remained standing beside it. "Your name is Tom?"

She waited a moment, then said, "Tommy, sit down, please."

He laughed at her. Contempt in his voice, he leaned across the table. "Her pet name for me won't work."

The guard took a step forward. "No."

The kid took a step back, eyes shifting from the guard to her and back. "She's dead, you know."

"I'm sorry, Tommy."

He snorted. "My name is Thirteen."

Britt nodded. "Okay." It had been worth a try. She now knew a lot more about the kid and his relationship to his dead mother than she had a minute ago. "Please have a seat, Thirteen."

He sat, slouched in his chair, laid his hands flat on the table, and fixed dark, unreadable eyes on a point somewhere above her left shoulder.

She leaned in a bit. "You must miss your mother."

A scowl, an expression of annoyance, flitted across his face. Then it was gone. He glanced at her. "You look at her picture?"

"No. I haven't seen it."

He reached out and tapped the manilla folder that lay in front of her. "Bet it's in there."

"I'll look at it later."

He grinned, showing perfect white teeth. "You better look now."

Part of her screamed no, but her hand was opening the kid's dossier.

He sat back and watched.

She leafed through the summary pages, which she'd just barely had time to skim, then turned to the next section, to an eight by ten photo of his mother. Her back was propped against the trunk of a tree, and her head lolled to one side.

Britt's heart nearly stopped. Shoulder-length light brown hair. A heart-shaped face with too long a nose and too wide a mouth. She was looking at a carbon copy of herself. Half-lying in a tangle of grass and weeds, the woman may have been slightly more slender, but about one hundred twenty-five pounds and probably the same height, five and a half feet. Except there was a knife sticking out of her chest and her hazel eyes stared blankly up at the sky.

Britt's head felt light. Her brain wasn't getting enough oxygen.

He leered at her. "See what I mean?"

She closed the file, took a breath, and reminded herself to keep both hands relaxed and open on the table. "Tell me about your mother."

"That's not going to work." The kid slumped back and stared at a spot somewhere behind her. "See, when interviewing a suspect, the first step is to establish rapport," he said, as if reading from a textbook. "That would not be talking about *her*. Then, once we get that out of the way, we can go on to the next part, where you empathize with me and let me know, subtly, of course, that maybe you can understand why I might kill my mother. Like, maybe I made a mistake. Maybe I thought she was a burglar or something. And then I'm supposed to break down and tell you all about how I took a knife from the kitchen and followed her into the park and deep into the woods, and just as the sun was setting, I plunged the knife into her heart."

"Did you?"

He sat up straight and stared into her eyes, scowling. "Why are you accusing me? What right do you have to say I would do that?"

"I only asked. Thirteen, I want to help you."

He snickered. "No, you don't. You're here because I wouldn't talk to that mad scientist."

"Do you mean Dr. Plitman?"

"No, I mean Santa Claus. Oscar Plitman. What a name! I bet he told you to come."

"He asked me to come."

"He thought maybe I'd talk to you because you look like her."

"Possibly."

"And then you could tell him all about it so he can write me up and give his brilliant analysis to the court."

Britt hesitated. It had been too long since she'd studied adolescents.

"See, I can tell you agree with me." He leaned over the table and put a finger to his lips. "Shhh. Don't worry. I'm not going to talk to you either."

The kid was bright. Bright and twisted.

He shoved his chair back and stood. He jerked his head toward the door. "Guard. I'm outta here."

Before the guard led him away, he aimed a smirk at her. "Nice meeting you." The contempt in his eyes chilled her to the bone.

It was as if a bolt of lightning passed between them. She knew he'd killed his mother and he knew she knew.

And they both knew he would probably get away with it.

****

Britt smacked Thirteen's dossier down on the pile of papers on Oscar Plitman's desk, then began pacing around his cluttered University of Washington office.

"Well, that was a boatload of fun."

Oscar gazed at her for a moment. "What's the problem?"

"The kid who calls himself Thirteen. He ran circles around me. I felt like an idiot."

"Good experience for you."

"I don't need the experience. Especially not *that* experience. The defense of my dissertation is tomorrow. What I need is time to prepare."

A ray of sun broke through the clouds and streamed in through the window. It gleamed off his high forehead and shone through his thin, wiry, gray hair, but left his pinched mouth and too-close together eyes marooned in the shadows. A metaphor for the man himself. She could never tell what was going on in that brilliant mind.

"Look, Brittie—"

"At least you could have told me I looked like his mother."

"I could have. But it would have changed your approach and your reactions."

She plopped into the hard oak chair facing his desk and let out a huge sigh. "True."

"Am I forgiven?"

"Only if you give me the job of analyzing your study on the causes of recidivism in males older than thirty."

He grinned. "I'm thinking about it. How would you like to be there when I present it at the International Conference on Deviant Behavior in Beijing in September?"

"Heck, yeah! I'd love it." She would stand beside him on the podium at this prestigious event. By then, she'd be Dr. Brittany Ann Thornton. It would be so amazing. It would leapfrog her career light years ahead.

With that on her resume, she'd be able to choose any job she wanted, and when it came to negotiating a salary, she'd have beaucoup bargaining power. She'd compete on Oscar's level for grant money. She'd do her own research.

Finally, she had her life all dialed in.

Chapter Two

Seattle

Naked, Britt curled her toes into the thick white carpet and frowned at herself in the full-length mirror. She turned sideways, grabbed the roll of fat at her waist, and gave it a little shake. Nope. Not even a smidge smaller. Twelve pounds. How hard could it be to lose twelve pounds?

Up until now, it had been impossible. But no worries. After today, she wouldn't have to juggle studying, working as a research assistant, and preparing to defend her dissertation while mothering an almost-teenage daughter and supporting her civic-minded businessman husband.

After today, she'd prepare healthy, nutritious meals. No more pizza deliveries. No more fast food. Best of all, no more stressed-out sleepless nights when the only thing that calmed her nerves was to sneak down to the kitchen and eat a handful of cookies while making lists of things to follow up on after the sun came up.

Britt turned back to the mirror and pulled up a strand of hair, something else she'd been neglecting. No more shoving it into a bun or ponytail. Time for a new style, a good cut. Maybe she'd get some highlights put in, something to bring out the hazel in her eyes and draw attention away from her mouth, which was too wide for her pointy chin. Yes. She'd get on it as soon as she got back from Paris.

Then she'd invite Rob to a dinner date—alone, just the two of them. They'd rekindle the romance that seemed to have disappeared from their marriage.

"Mo-o-m!" Megan's voice, tinged with a sort of resigned exasperation, carried up the stairs. "Would you please hurry up? Grandma and I are going to miss our plane."

Omigod!

How had she managed to produce a child who insisted on punctuality? Megan would be dressed in her best jeans, meaning the ones with the most holes, so she could look ultra-cool for her trip to California, and ready to go.

Britt snatched up her bra. Usually, she didn't care what she wore, as long as it hid that evil roll of fat. But today, because she faced the defense of her dissertation, she struggled into a pair of tights.

Five minutes later, she twisted her hair into a knot at the back of her head, swiped some lipstick on, and sucked in her stomach so she could button the waistband of her skirt. Pulling on her new camel blazer, she slid her feet into her good pumps and headed for the family room, where she felt pretty sure she'd left her laptop.

Cynthia Thornton, her mother, and Megan had already loaded their suitcases in the back of the car. They waited by the door, her mother with a little grin on her face, Megan scowling. Britt patted her arm. "Honey, you'll be fine. You'll get there in plenty of time."

Driving a little too fast, but not fast enough to invite a speeding ticket, Britt headed for the light rail. Thank goodness she didn't have to take them all the way to the airport.

At the University station, she helped them drag their suitcases out of the trunk, then hugged her mother. Megan was already halfway to the escalator. Britt sighed. Megan had been born with a thing about being on time. Just then, she turned around and blew a kiss, and Britt felt as if the sun had broken through the clouds. Grinning, she blew one back.

Still smiling, she jumped back into her car. After twenty-five years of nonstop school, this was her last day as a student, and she wasn't going to let anything spoil it. Not the fact that she was nearly fifteen minutes late, not the gray Seattle mist, not even the image of Thirteen's mother, propped against the tree trunk with a knife in her chest. Every time it flashed into her mind, she shoved it right back out. Today, she would not rent space in her head to anything with a negative value.

Tonight, she and Rob would celebrate with Arielle, her best friend since first grade, over dinner in Pike Place Market. Arielle would insist on buying a bottle of expensive champagne, and Britt was not going to argue.

****

Oscar, bless him, wrapped up Britt's defense a little after three o'clock. He was in a hurry to get home to his rose garden.

She had a standing date for a tennis lesson at four-thirty and had forgotten to call and cancel it. How fab was that? There was just enough time to nip home and grab her racquet. She was done with school at last. Megan was already in California with her grandma. For the first time in years, Britt had nothing to do but play and dress for dinner.

At home, almost before the wheels stopped turning, she leaped out of the car and dashed up the driveway, holding the umbrella over her laptop. Good thing the tennis club had indoor courts. She tapped in the code on the keypad by the front door and pushed it open. The faint scent of lemony furniture polish told her the house cleaner had been there that morning. Excellent! She plopped her computer down on the narrow table below the hall mirror and opened the closet. Her racquet lay on the shelf above the coats. As her fingers closed around the handle, she stiffened.

Rob had always been a creative, energetic, and vocal lover. And she knew exactly what each moan, sigh, and cry meant. Shaking, heart pounding, Britt launched herself up the stairs, gripping the handle of her racquet as hard as she could.

He hadn't even closed the door.

From the doorway, she glimpsed a high, proud, button-sized breast. Long, firm thighs spread to accommodate her husband's trim, muscular hips. They were making so much noise she could have herded in a bunch of bleating, smelly goats and they wouldn't have noticed. For a moment, she stood there, transfixed.

Then something snapped. Britt sprang across the thick white carpet, raised the racquet, and slammed it down on Rob's naked butt, wanting with all her might to drive it right through him.

He rolled over and started to sit up.

She jumped back. "How dare you?"

Never in her life had she ever felt this way—wild, strong, invincible. The racquet sang on the upswing. It had never sounded so sweet.

Poised to strike again, Britt caught herself. *Omigod.* Crimes of passion. That was how they happened. What was she thinking? She gulped in a breath and lowered the racquet.

He scrambled off the bed, grabbed it, and wrenched it out of her hand. "Aren't you surprised at yourself, Brittany? Stooping to hit another person?" He threw it across the room. It hit the mirrored closet door and shattered the glass.

"Rob, get her out of here."

Britt froze. Her husband's partner had pulled the sheet over her face, but Britt knew that voice. The girl next door, whose mother had died when she was five. The reality of it stunned her, took her breath away. For a long moment, she could only stare at the invisible form.

Then she snatched a handful of the sheet and yanked. "You! Go! Get out of my house. I never, ever want to see you again."

Graciella Cordova rolled off the far side of the bed and stood, unafraid and unashamed. "God, sweetie. I thought you said she was busy." She shook long black hair until it cascaded to her slender waist and lifted tiny but lovely breasts.

"Get out." Britt's voice broke. It didn't belong to her anymore, but kept on screaming, "Get out—get out—get out. You horrid, nasty, filthy little bitch."

Rob glanced at his lover, then back at her. "Britt, look—"

"You promised," she shrieked. *"You promised!"*

He reached out and touched her arm. Her husband, always strong and steady. "Britt."

Suddenly, the rage died. The fury drained down through her feet, down through the carpet, down into the earth, until nothing was left. All her strength went with it, and she could barely stand. "You promised," she whispered.

Her heart had never hurt this hard before. "You promised you would never do this again, and I believed you." She raised her head and looked at Graciella. "And you. How could you? I have taken care of you all these years. I have treated you like a daughter."

Graciella, haughty and contemptuous, stared back. "Oh, wow, I am so not your daughter."

Britt's heart hammered at her ribs. "How many times have I driven you to practice, school, or the mall? How many sandwiches have I made for you? How many birthday cakes and pots of spaghetti?" She pulled herself up tall and met Graciella's defiant gaze. "You are quite right. I do not know you."

She glared at Rob. "Nor do I know you, you lying sack of shit. What do you mean screwing her? She's only five years older than Megan, for heaven's sake. How long have you been mucking about right here in my bed? Did you even wait until she turned eighteen?"

Anger propelled her out of the house, back to the car, around the corners, and down the streets to the tennis club. Not knowing how she got there, she pulled into the first vacant parking place and tried to dam the tears that poured down her face.

If only she'd taken her racquet with her this morning, she wouldn't know. It wouldn't hurt.

Chapter Three

Seattle

A few blocks from downtown, Pike Place Market, Seattle's iconic farmers' market, clung to the hillside above the waterfront. At the entrance, Britt stood beside the famous pig, a thigh-high, five-hundred-fifty-pound brass piggy bank that collected donations for social services in the neighborhood. Normally, she would have dropped some money in and rubbed its nose for luck, but today she didn't even see it.

Just steps away, fish mongers in rubber boots and orange rubber overalls shouted orders as they pulled whole, large, silvery fish out of bins of ice and sent them flying through the air to teammates. They wrapped the fish, and then, while the omnipresent crowd laughed, yelled, and cheered, tossed them to waiting customers. Oblivious to the distinctive odor of flying salmon, the tourists snapping photos, and the people milling around her, Britt waited.

She stared out at the rain slanting down under the streetlights, unaware that her new leather pumps were soaking up water and not caring that her best blazer was no match for the chill spring air. Arielle was fifteen minutes late, but Britt didn't so much as glance at her phone.

A few hours earlier, she'd been on top of the

world, but now, it took every ounce of energy to keep Rob's infidelity from overwhelming her, from making her want to lie down and die. Her body felt rigid, brittle, and she knew that heartache wasn't just an expression, as she'd always thought. Her heart actually hurt.

Finally, aware of the chill, she turned away from the street and looked down the long center aisle of the market. A platinum blonde head bobbed in and out of the throng, moving slowly in her direction. A tiny point of light kindled in the darkness.

Late as usual, Arielle McGregor wasn't hurrying. She never hurried, and somehow that made her gait look elegant. She limped out of the crowd, taupe trench coat open to reveal a soft gray-blue knit dress that matched her eyes and clung to her body. She was, as always stunning: model thin, model tall, model gorgeous. And as always, she seemed oblivious to the way people turned and looked at her. She carried a huge, multicolored market bouquet in the crook of one elbow. A wide smile lit her face. "You wouldn't answer your phone, and I couldn't wait to hear, so I called Oscar. He told me your defense of your dissertation was brilliant. Congratulations!"

Britt bit her lip. Had she been brilliant?

Arielle hugged her hard. "Dinner's on me. I made reservations. Where's Rob?"

"Rob who?"

Arielle stepped back. Her eyebrows went up, and her mouth dropped open. She peered at Britt's face. "Omigod. What's going on? You look awful."

Britt took a deep breath. "Did you know he's been having an affair?" Her voice cracked, but she ignored it. Tears pressed against her eyelids. "Did you?"

Arielle's forehead wrinkled in concern. "Why didn't I tell you; that's what you're asking, isn't it?"

Unable to speak, she nodded. She gazed at her friend, certain that she was the last to know.

"I didn't know." Arielle reached out and took her hand. "I'm not sure I would have told you if I had, but I didn't."

"But you're not surprised."

"I—"

A gust of wind whipped in. Britt shivered.

"Come on. You're freezing." Arielle nudged her away from the pig, then past the crowd around the fish market. As they headed toward the vegetable stalls, she drew a deep breath. "I'm not surprised. Not really. I'm sorry to say that." She paused. "I've wondered."

Hail slammed down on the roof. All around them, people grinned, pointed at the little white stones bouncing off the brick pavers in the street, and raised their voices to be heard above the noise.

Britt paid no attention. "You've wondered. Explain."

"Well, it's not the first time. And some of our friends have talked."

"About what?"

"Nothing specific."

"What does that mean?"

"That you hardly ever show up in the same car, or at the same time, things like that."

Britt clutched her arm and turned to face her. "I see. Everyone's been talking, and even though you've been in Europe, on an entirely different continent, you heard." People jostled against them as they pushed past on both sides. "Everyone heard. I should have known.

You think I should have known."

"No." Arielle shook her head. "Shit, Britt, you had no way to know. Don't cry." She fished a linen handkerchief out of her coat pocket. "Here, take my hanky." She tucked it into her hand. "Seriously, I'd give anything to not see you hurt this way."

"I caught him with Graciella this afternoon."

"Omigod." The color drained from Arielle's face. "Omigod."

"Honest. Promise me you didn't know."

"No. Holy cow. No." She tugged Britt over to the side, next to an olive oil stall, out of the flow of traffic. "Why, in the name of God and all the angels, didn't you call me right away?"

"I couldn't talk about it."

Arielle thrust the flowers into Britt's hands. "He deserves major pain. I'm going to buy a voodoo doll and jab sharp pins into his nasty little bits." She pulled her phone out of her purse. "Look, I can't bear to see you go through this again. I'm going to send you Viktor's number right now."

"Viktor?"

"I know, I know, he's my ex." She swiped the screen, tapped, swiped again, and then dropped the phone back into her purse. "He's also the best divorce lawyer around. And he's always liked you."

"But what about Megan? She's at a terrible age for parents to split, and she adores her father."

"And she's my godchild. And I will do anything I can to help. Bottom line, you can't stay with someone who treats you this way."

Britt wiped up tears. "I know. I went back to the house to tell him, but I couldn't do it. He was in the shower, and he was whistling *Tennessee Waltz*."

Arielle hugged her. "You're going to be okay. I promise. And next week, you're coming to Paris with me, as planned."

"How can I do that now? I'm going to have to stay here and deal with this mess."

"Let Viktor handle it. You don't have to speak to Rob ever again if you don't want to."

Britt tried to smile. "Maybe."

"Definitely." Arielle peered out into the gloom. "It's stopped hailing. The storm is letting up. Come on. Let's hustle over to the restaurant. Right this minute, a glass of champagne is absolutely required. I can't imagine how you've survived this long without it."

"Alcohol does not solve problems."

Arielle's arm tightened around her shoulders. "You sound like a Sunday school teacher with inflamed bunions."

Britt leaned against her. "I'm glad you're back—I think."

Chapter Four

Paris, France

Viane Thibaudet stood in front of the long oval mirror and scrutinized her image. Her body looked fine. Her hair and makeup were perfect, as was the chic black dress waiting on the hanger. But the eyes that looked back at her belonged to the girl who came to school with bruises on her arms, the girl in worn shoes and threadbare dresses, the girl who didn't belong.

In that backward little village where she grew up, she would never be anyone else, no matter what she accomplished. Even though she was the one who had put Chevalier on the map. They were proud of her, the townspeople said. Peasants. All of them. A bunch of sheep. Content to play boules on Saturday and go to mass every Sunday.

She slid her feet into soft leather mules, shrugged into her silk kimono, and headed for the espresso machine in the kitchen.

For the last three years, she had shuttled back and forth between Paris and Chevalier. She had slaved—slaved—to simultaneously build the clientele in Provence and develop a reputation in Paris as a chef. Now she had the option to buy the *Cochon Qui Rit*, a two-star restaurant near the Eiffel Tower. But Jean-Luc expected her to stay home in Provence and bear a brood of snotty brats. Damn his provincial hubris!

While she waited for the espresso machine to warm up, she recalled the way Jean-Luc's father died. It had been in her mind often lately.

Holding his plate, Gaspard Thibaudet stretched out his hand. He took three steps toward her before he stumbled, and the plate slid out of his fingers. Three steps before he gasped out, "Viane!"

Three steps before his knees buckled and he crumpled to the terrace. In slow motion, the plate hit the flagstones, bounced, and shattered, just as his head cracked down on the unforgiving stone.

The guests hushed and turned, staring open-mouthed toward the fallen man. Jean-Luc knelt beside his father, turning him to his back. He shook his shoulder and shouted, "Papa, Papa, Papa," and then, "Viane, telephone for help."

Viane scooped the coffee in and turned the espresso machine on.

When her husband's mother, Martine Thibaudet, died three months later, everyone said it was because of a broken heart, obviously. Except Viane's own mother, who looked at her with eyes full of doubt and suspicion.

Jean-Luc inherited his parents' farm and his grandmother's large estate, including the house in Paris, which she loved. He did not care for the city. He only wanted to stay in Provence and milk his wonderful, revered cows. Fine. Let him stay.

In a couple of days, she would go back to Chevalier. She'd try again to convince him to help her buy the restaurant she wanted with every cell in her body.

She would have it. She had worked too hard to let

it slip out of her grasp. Watching the rich, dark coffee stream into her cup, she hugged her arms to her chest and felt the first giddy, exultant rush of success.

She was meant for rue Saint-Dominique, the cover of *Haute Cuisine de Paris* magazine, and Michelin stars. If she hesitated, she would miss her chance. Someone else would buy the *Cochon Qui Rit*, someone with ready money. And all of Paris would know that in spite of her prosperous image, she was just a poor girl in a threadbare dress.

****

Chevalier, Provence, France

Jacqueline Thibaudet leaned forward in the seat and peered at her father's face. "Viane must be awfully good at sex."

Jean-Luc Thibaudet caught his breath. He focused on the road while he considered what to say. He accelerated to pass his neighbor, Didier, sitting tall on his old blue tractor with the dent in the fender, and slowed again before he glanced at his offspring.

"Is that why you married her, Papa?"

Jean-Luc opened and closed his mouth, but no words came out. He cleared his throat. "This is not a question that fathers discuss with their children, Jacqueline." The words sounded harsh, and he didn't intend them to be. "Why do you ask such a question?" It was amusing, once he had a moment to consider it. Weren't children such a surprise?

"Is this a modern trend?"

"I don't know why you married her. That's all."

"Ah, I see." He did see, all too well, although he preferred not to. Jacqueline was picking at his one area of discontent, the part of his life that always seemed tilted to one side, the part where he felt consistently off balance.

"Yes. Viane is very messy. She leaves her clothes and shoes in the living room. You don't like me to do that, but she always does. And she never hangs up her towel properly in the bathroom. And lots of times she goes to Paris and stays there at Grandmama's house with Marcel. So, she must be good at sex or you wouldn't have married her."

"I see."

"Was my mother like that?"

"*Ma Petite*! Such a question!"

"I mean, was she messy?"

"Your mother was not messy." He looked in the mirror, hoping to hide his smile. "Your mother liked to make everything pretty. She kept the house tidy and clean. The furniture shone, and the floors always gleamed with wax. She loved to bring in flowers from the garden." He took a deep breath. Sometimes, he missed her still. Sometimes, the ache in his heart reminded him how much he had lost. But didn't he have Jacqueline? He smiled at her. "We did not have much money, but she knew how to put together pleasant colors and how to make our house happy and comfortable."

"I wish I could see her. I look at her photograph, and I try to see what she would be like if she were here with us, but I can't."

"I see her every day, *Ma Petite*, every time I look at you. Sometimes it stops my breath. You are so like her." Jean-Luc's throat closed. He couldn't continue.

"I wish she didn't die."

"*Ah, oui, Ma Petite. Moi aussi.* It was very hard to go on without her." He took his eyes off the road to study his child. The expression on her face was one he had seen often lately; pensive, lonely, and something else—waiting perhaps.

"Do you wish you didn't marry her?" she asked. "Why *did* you?"

He shifted down, slowed to cross the bridge over the stream, then turned up the hill to Chevalier. "You were so little. We both missed your mother so much. And then one day, Viane came back from the Sorbonne. Her dream was to buy the bistro and make wonderful food for our town." He turned into the narrow street that wound upward toward the town square. Viane had been so beautiful, and so wistful. She had no money. Her mother had no money. How would she be able to make her dream come true?

"I felt so alone. I thought Viane would be a good mother and that you would have brothers and sisters." He was still alone. Except for Jacqueline.

They had reached the town square. "Time to set up for the market," he said, backing the truck and putting on the brake. Jacqueline pulled her long dark hair into a ponytail and snapped a rubber band around it, and by the time he turned off the engine, she had opened the door and slid out the far side of the truck.

Chapter Five

Paris

Britt and Arielle arrived in Paris a little after seven in the morning, following a ten-hour flight from Seattle. Britt wanted to brush her teeth and crawl into bed, but Arielle had booked a tour to Giverny. "If we stay up until normal bedtime," she said, "we won't have jetlag." They drank double espressos, got on a bus, and spent the afternoon admiring Monet's famous waterlily ponds and gardens. Back in Paris that evening, they ate duck confit for dinner and topped it off with a rich, silky crème brulée. Then, finally, it was time to prop themselves up in their beds and read their novels.

Britt's phone chimed with an incoming text message. A smiling selfie of the kid who called himself Thirteen popped up.

—I hear you are Doctor Thornton now. Congratulations.—

His cocky grin jolted her right back to that ghastly interview with him at the juvenile detention center. Chills ran down her back.

She forwarded the message to Oscar Plitman. It was morning in Seattle, and her mentor was an early bird, so when he didn't respond immediately, she phoned him. The minute he accepted the call, she realized she had been holding her breath. "Oscar, I *know* Thirteen killed his mother, and now he has my phone number. It's creeping me out."

"You can't possibly know he's responsible for her murder. The police couldn't find a single shred of hard evidence."

"That doesn't mean he didn't do it."

"The kid isn't exactly a model citizen, but I don't see anything threatening in the message he sent you."

"You don't look like his mother, who is dead, by the way."

"Point taken. I can see why you're upset. He's on parole for car theft, so I'll get his parole officer's number for you. You should forward the message to him. But don't worry. You've seen his MMPI scores, and they don't point him out as a killer."

"So, scales four and nine are not outrageous. But they *are* elevated."

"Not enough to cause alarm."

"Then there's the history of drowning kittens."

"According to a neighbor. It was not corroborated by evidence, and no one else supported that accusation."

"Okay, so nobody cares what I think. Nobody actually wanted my evaluation. Why didn't I just submit my grocery list? I could have saved myself a boatload of trouble."

Oscar was right, of course. There was no way she could know the kid had killed his mother, and the police had found no evidence. Britt tossed the phone to the foot of the bed and flopped down on her pillow.

From her bed a few feet away, Arielle looked up from her book. "Think about it from Oscar's point of view. If that kid had confessed to you that he killed his mother, he would have scored a coup by sending you."

"I wish he had levelled with me. Sometimes I think he's trying to keep me tamped down in my old place as his student."

"I don't think he would do that, at least not consciously. But at some point, you're going to be competing with him for recognition, which means grant money, and you may very well eclipse him. He's got to be aware of that."

"You think I have to toughen up."

Arielle smiled. "I think you need to protect your heart. Trust your instincts. Believe in your own value. And stop worrying about what other people, including Oscar, think."

Britt sighed. The night breeze lifted the pale, gauzy curtain away from the French door and drifted with welcome coolness over her arms and face. By the ambient light, she could see the geraniums in the planter on the minuscule balcony. Beyond that, above tile roofs, the top of the Eiffel Tower glowed like a diamond tiara.

A woman's heels clicked along the street, and her laughter drifted up on a puff of air, the sound of a lover in love, as light and supple as the song of a meadowlark. Britt used to laugh like that. How long ago! She got up, stepped over the sill onto the balcony, and peered down through the bright red geraniums at rue Cler. The unseen woman's laughter faded away to the right.

Britt's long white cotton gown swirled away from her legs. She hugged her arms to her chest and wondered if Viktor had delivered the divorce papers to Rob yet. She hadn't been able to fix her marriage any more than she could keep Thirteen in jail.

Stop! Enough about that. Here she was in the City of Light at last. Time enough to think about Rob when she got home.

She stood there, watching the lighthouse beam at the top of the tower and listening to delivery trucks rumble down the cobbled street, the sound of Paris at night, until she felt chilled.

Shivering, she stepped back over the sill and slipped into bed. When she caught Rob with Graciella, for a moment, she had wanted with every fiber in her body to do serious bodily harm. She had hit him as hard as she could. She drifted to sleep wondering, was that what happened to Thirteen? Did he just suddenly lose it and plunge a knife into his mother's heart? Was she so different?

Chapter Six

Paris

Britt had barely opened her eyes the next morning when her daughter's image popped up on her phone. Megan was in full rant, with all the righteousness a not-quite-teenage girl could generate. "Dad said we have to sell the house and that I have to live with you—in a *condo*! How am I going to have any *privacy*? How am I going to have Rena and Naomi and Tiffany stay over *in a condo?*"

Megan's lips pulled into a thin line. Her dark blue eyes, so like her father's that Britt wanted to turn away, blazed at her across all those miles.

Nothing Britt said made the slightest difference.

"You are so, like, *totally* ruining my life. You are leaving me no option. You are *forcing* me. I am going to have to stay in California with grandma *permanently*." Her hand, still chubby and childish, loomed large in the screen. She tapped the touchpad, and her image disappeared. The cyber-equivalent of running to her room and slamming the door.

A cloud of steam emerged from the bathroom, and Arielle materialized in the midst of it, her hair wrapped in a towel, her body wrapped in her taupe silk dressing gown. "Your turn." She tipped her head to the side and looked at Britt. "Uh-oh. I see a stormy brow."

"I lost my patience with Megan."

"Forgot to put on your supermom cloak?"

"Apparently, living in a condo is akin to living in a refugee camp. It is beneath her. Sometimes I think I'm raising an ungrateful, self-centered little snob."

Arielle unwrapped the towel from her head and began to rub her hair. "The problem is, she's almost thirteen. When she's, like, *totally older,* Megan will be fine." She grinned. "Come on, get ready, and I'll buy you a croissant. You'll love the spa."

When they stepped out into the street, Britt stopped, closed her eyes, and took in a long, slow breath. "The whole place smells like butter and chocolate."

Arielle's laughter always sounded like liquid silver to Britt. It had lightened the trials that came their way ever since grade school. Now, still, when Arielle laughed, Britt's heart lifted.

They sat elbow to elbow at a tiny round outdoor table, facing the street. Men and women strode by wearing black suits, the women with red or blue or yellow silk scarves at the neck, smart, thin briefcases swinging from their hands, feet in pumps with heels, like Arielle's. Britt's navy pantsuit, her favorite all through grad school, felt frumpy.

She hid her feet in their flat, sturdy sandals under the table. "I definitely need to go shopping."

They cradled large white cups of *café crème* in their hands and savored airy, golden-crusted croissants, and then they strolled to the Eiffel Tower, slowly, so that Arielle's limp, the result of a motorcycle accident, was barely noticeable. They paused to look up at the mighty beams and marvel at how the structure soared so gracefully all the way to the top.

When they reached the Seine, Arielle hailed a taxi to take them to the spa.

At the reception desk in the spa's marble foyer, Britt's credit card would not go through. She dialed the number on the back of the card and verified her identity.

After a long pause, a young male voice said, "Ma'am, there is a hold on this account."

Britt frowned. "I don't understand."

"I am unable to access any information about this account."

"But I called and reported that I would be in France."

"That may be true, but I can't access your information. Please call again later."

Britt handed the receptionist her debit card instead. "Put it on this one, then."

That card didn't work either.

Britt frowned. "I don't understand. The ATM gave me euros last night, no problem."

She phoned her bank and explained. After an even longer wait, the customer service rep came back on. "I'm sorry, but I can't find your account."

Britt's grip tightened on her phone. "Why?"

"I can't bring it up on the computer."

"*Seriously*? I'm in Paris. I need to use my debit card."

"I'm sorry, ma'am." The woman's voice sounded young, smooth, and unconcerned. "It may be a temporary glitch. Please call back later."

"Wait, I need—" The line went dead. Britt bit her lip to keep from screaming.

Arielle put a hand on her arm. "Rob must have closed them."

Telling herself to breathe through the tightness, Britt shook her head. "I can't believe he would be that vindictive."

"Don't worry. Viktor will sort him out." Arielle handed her card over. "Put it on mine."

But Britt felt wobbly, the way she did as a kid learning to ride a bicycle, not sure she could keep her balance.

The woman Arielle called the Mud Bath Matron helped her settle into a tub of warm, silky mud, mildly fragrant with the scent of lavender. After a few seconds, she found that she floated, warm, weightless, and totally supported. She blew out a long breath. Arielle was right. It was silly to worry. Viktor would know what to do.

In the meantime, this was her first real vacation in a decade. And Arielle had promised that she'd love this very expensive spa, so she'd better enjoy it. She began to drift away.

Mud Bath Matron's voice came from somewhere above her starched pink bosom, "By the time you are leaving, your body will glow."

When a soft chime awakened her, the same woman was there to pry Britt out. It took a double espresso and a chunk of dark chocolate to get her upright again. Wrapped in a peach-colored robe, she sat in a room with many mirrors, and tall, lean, sexy Louis cut her hair. "Your hair is fine and shiny, like silk, Madame. And I have cut it to match the shape of your face." His warm, soft hand cupped her chin. "May I suggest that your beauty would be enhanced by this color?" He pointed at a color chart with the razor he still held.

"Red?"

"*Mais, non, non*, this color, it is called ginger. It is perfect for you. Only look. The color would be stunning with your eyes—hazel they are called, *n'est-ce pas?*"

When it was done, she could hardly stop looking at herself.

Arielle, fully dressed, showed up and peered at her for a long moment, then said, "Ooh-la-la." She blew a kiss. "I'm off to work now. See you tonight at the hotel."

A young woman with a spiked purple Mohawk applied warm, coral-toned makeup, painted Britt's nails a soft peachy color, and then led her to a full-length mirror. She barely recognized the person who stared back at her. A softer, brighter, and, yes, much sexier woman.

Back in her navy pantsuit, Britt floated around the corner onto the Champs-Elysées. She paused to admire a dress in a window. And her reflection. As the Mud Bath Matron had promised, she glowed. Thirty minutes later, she emerged from the shop wearing a scoop-necked black dress and four-inch leopard heels. She tucked a leopard clutch purse, long and slim like Arielle's, under her arm.

As silly as it was to walk down this famous street in brand-new shoes, risking brand-new blisters, she had to do it. Another block, she told herself. Another block to feel totally feminine. Another block of feeling deliciously alive and sexy. And hungry. A magenta awning shading little round tables and striped magenta chairs invited her in. She had run out of cash, well, almost. But no worries. Viktor was on it. She slid into a chair facing the street and ordered pâté and champagne.

She sipped, felt the bubbles tingle on her tongue. It was a watercolor moment, as if painted by Renoir—*Luncheon of the Transformation of Brittany Ann Thornton.* This day, with this exact combination of events, would never come again. She would savor every second.

Since it was after the normal lunch hour and the place was half-empty, it seemed odd that a man in a blue polo shirt and tan pants chose the very next table.

He leaned toward her. "Refreshing to find a fellow American so far off the beaten boulevard."

Was he hitting on her? Amazing. "The Champs-Elysées," she said, pointing, "is only ten feet away."

"Most tourists go to the Eiffel Tower, then take a ride on a *bateau mouche,* and never get all the way over here. If they do, it's on a tour bus with an audio guide that spews out ten languages. But here you are all by yourself, and you've been shopping."

"Yes, well, I guess I'm not most tourists." *And I didn't sleep much last night, and this champagne is making my head fuzzy, and I wish you would just go away.*

"Indeed, you are not."

Why did he look familiar? A medium man. Medium height, medium weight, medium age, brown hair curling a little around his ears, brown eyes behind small rectangular glasses. Ahhh. She had seen him this morning, near the Eiffel Tower, when she and Arielle got in the taxi.

"My lower-than-pond-scum husband hired you to follow me, didn't he?"

He reached into a pocket and pulled out a wallet.

"Stan Gibson. I work for the FBI."

"The FBI? In Paris? You expect me to believe that? What kind of scam is this?"

He offered his credentials for inspection. "No scam at all. FBI agents are attached to American embassies all over the world. We protect American interests and assist with solving and preventing international criminal schemes."

"And you're following me because?"

"My colleagues in Seattle are wondering what you know about two-and-a-half million dollars that have gone missing from your account at TD Sterling."

Britt held up a hand. "Look, I don't know what you're playing at, but this isn't funny. I don't have an account at TD Sterling."

He scrutinized her face. "Washington is a community property state, and your husband has an account. Therefore, you do, or, I should say, *you did.*"

Britt felt her heart rate pick up. Her mouth went dry. "No."

"Yes."

She stared at him. "With two-and-a-half million dollars? Who are you kidding?"

He shrugged. "It's intriguing, see, that you left the country two days ago, right when the money disappeared. And now, all of a sudden, you look quite different." He held up a copy of *Who Lies and Why,* one of the books she had co-authored with Oscar Plitman.

Her photograph gazed at her from the back cover. Fifteen pounds lighter, a little skinny, actually. No makeup. Mousy hair pulled back in a clip at the nape of her neck.

He said, "You don't much resemble your picture."

Britt's heart started to thump against her ribs. "That was five years ago."

"Yeah, okay. But today you could pass for a different person." He squinted his eyes and wagged his head from side to side a couple of times, as if to say, "Terribly silly of me, I know."

"Is that look meant to disarm me?"

"Yeah, sort of. Tell me, you wouldn't be thinking about leaving the country, would you? Maybe heading off to parts unknown?"

She glared at him. "I get it. You think I cleaned out this alleged account and absconded with the alleged money, and now I'm planning to turn up somewhere else with a new identity."

"Forgive my suspicious mind, but it's what I get paid for. That much money could take you a long way."

"*If* I had this account, then it would be my money to start with. Why would anyone, let alone the FBI, care?"

Her phone quacked like a duck. She pulled it out of her purse. Please, let it be Viktor. Yes. Thank God. She held up a finger. "I need to take this call." She got up and walked toward the street as she answered.

Viktor didn't even say hello. "Britt, sorry about your credit cards. It may take a few days to get some money freed up for you."

"Why?"

"Haven't you heard?"

"What?"

"Are you sitting down?"

"Just, for God's sake, tell me."

"Rob was arrested late yesterday afternoon. The FBI has frozen your accounts and assets."

"Why?" Her knees started to shake. "What is going on?" She peered back over her shoulder at Stan Gibson.

"It's part of a widespread takedown by the FBI's Medicare Fraud Task Force. Rob is one of twenty-three indicted."

Britt headed back to her table. "But Viktor, they investigated Thornton Medical months ago. They found nothing. They closed the case."

"At this time, that's all I know."

Dread clasped her heart in a cold fist. She collapsed into her chair. "So that's why my credit card won't work, or my debit card."

"Exactly. You'll remember that I counseled you to set up your own individual accounts."

She lifted a shaking hand to her brow, slippery with cold perspiration. She must not vomit on the table. She must not.

"You did." She dragged in a deep breath. "But that doesn't help me now."

"I can wire you some funds, a loan against the divorce settlement, until I get this sorted out."

"I'll let you know if I need you to do that."

"Good. Hang tough. I'm on it."

"Viktor, there's this man—" she began, but her lawyer had rung off.

When she finally turned back to FBI agent Gibson, she saw a hint of sympathy in his eyes. It was the last thing she wanted. Exactly the last thing. She bit her lip to keep from crying, then drew a deep breath. "I don't have what you're looking for. In fact, I don't know anything about it, or even if it ever actually existed. Please go away. You can stop following me."

"One more thing. You are the owner of Thornton

Medical, provider of medically necessary equipment such as wheelchairs, are you not?"

"No. Well, yes. My father left it to me in his will. But I, personally, have never had anything to do with operations."

"So, who runs it?"

"My ex-husband managed it before Dad died and has ever since."

"Robin Fitzroy Glance, your husband."

"Ex. And he goes by 'Rob'."

His eyes, brown if they really were brown, stared into hers. "Not yet an *ex*."

She stared back. "I have no money. I have done nothing wrong. This conversation is finished. If you have questions, you can talk to my attorney."

"Ah, yes, the invincible Viktor di Presti. The man is a shark."

"I think I need a shark."

Chapter Seven

Paris

Britt watched Agent Stan Gibson thread his way between the tables and disappear into the crowd on the Champs-Élysées. Then she leaned her elbows on the little round table and hid her face in her hands. She felt like something the cat had dragged in. Her not-yet-ex, Rob, indicted for fraud. How could that be? Please, God, make it a giant mistake.

Her father, Theo Thornton, had always expected everyone to be as honest and ethical as he. As a kid, Britt had never been able to get away with lying or cheating. He'd grounded her for even the tiniest offenses.

As founder of Thornton Medical Equipment, Theo had drummed his principles into his employees, including Rob, whom he hired and later promoted to manager. A little voice insisted on reminding her that her dad had hired him because, at nineteen, she was pregnant and determined to marry the twenty-seven-year-old ski instructor. She tried to ignore it. The promotion meant her dad approved of Rob, didn't it? So, when he died, Britt had given her husband free rein to carry on running the company.

But if he owned a secret account with two-and-a-half million dollars in it, that was way more than he could have earned in the six years he'd been in control. Could he have embezzled that much? Not likely. The company didn't bring in enough to make that feasible. That left fraudulent Medicare claims the most likely source of the alleged nest egg. Fraud. Just as this Stan Gibson said.

To pull something of that magnitude off, Rob would have had to conspire with at least a couple of doctors, probably some nurses and therapists, and the billing staff. Twenty-three people, Viktor said. Huge. It must include all four equipment and supply stores in the Thornton chain.

Back in January, the inspectors had audited Thornton Medical's books. They said they'd found nothing. But if this was true, then they were bluffing. They were just keeping quiet until they had enough evidence to arrest everybody.

All that time, Britt had plowed ahead with her research on married couples and the lies they tell each other. She watched hundreds of people interacting with their spouses, captured both verbal and nonverbal expressions on video, and then analyzed it all. And never once suspected that Rob was screwing both the federal government and the girl from next door.

She was an idiot. Interpersonal communication, spoken and unspoken—that was her specialty, her area of expertise. She should have figured it out.

Oscar had. Now she understood why he referred to her dissertation as *"How to Know if Your Husband is Cheating on You,"* as if it were a joke. Thank God she didn't have to be around him right now. He wouldn't be able to resist rubbing her nose in it—subtly, of course.

Slowly, with growing dread, she got to her feet and

gathered her parcels. She would walk back to the hotel. She had too few euros left to squander on a taxi. Until Viktor restored access to her bank account, she would have to borrow from Arielle. When Arielle's second husband died, he left her enough cash to finance Scotland, Ireland, and half of England, so that wasn't a problem. But Britt choked on the idea of feeling dependent, even temporarily.

She trudged out onto the sidewalk. Earlier, she had been thrilled to be part of the throng walking down this chic, bustling boulevard with its sleek window displays, but now it felt crowded and unfriendly. Everybody was rushing. People jostled against her. Britt walked faster.

Eager to find a quiet place, she turned onto a narrow side street. At first, it felt better, but after a few blocks, she found that she'd lost her sense of direction. The road twisted first one way and then another. It intersected with other streets at odd angles. She squinted at the sky, hoping to spot the sun without luck. She tried to retrace her steps, but all the buildings looked the same. She shifted her parcels from one hand to the other. She stumbled on a curb and nearly fell. She wished with all her might that she'd hit Rob a whole lot harder when she caught him with Graciella Cordova.

At last, by chance, she glimpsed one of the ornate gold statues above the Alexander III bridge. With a sigh of relief, she headed toward it. A few minutes later, she crossed over the Seine and finally found rue Cler. Another obstacle, a huge forest-green sedan, all four corners flashing lights, had pulled right up to the door of the hotel and almost blocked the entrance. *Huh! Who rates this monstrosity?*

She had exhausted her patience, and her feet in the

smart leopard stilettos hurt like holy heck. One extra step was one too many. She edged around it, wanting desperately to kick a shiny new fender.

"Ah, *voila*!" In the cool, dim interior, the woman at the hotel desk beckoned to Britt. "This gentleman waits for you."

A tall man in an impeccable black wool suit stood beside the tiny glass elevator. He was gorgeous. Black hair swept back from his face and caressed his collar. Enormous dark eyes set in an olive-toned face regarded her with languorous curiosity. He stepped toward her.

Britt's eyes widened. "Has the airline sent the suitcase they lost?" If the airline had sent her bag, why didn't he just leave it? And why would a courier dress in a thousand-dollar suit?

"*Non*," the woman at the desk said. "Madame Arielle McGregor telephoned that she is sending Madame Thibaudet's chauffeur for you."

His thick black eyebrows twitched upward above his strong, arched nose, and he smiled, looking amused. "I have come to bring you to the studio," he said in a smooth Italian accent.

Eye candy that sounds like heaven. This could not be happening to her. "Studio?"

"*Oui*." He started toward the exit. "It is where Madame McGregor is now working with Madame Thibaudet. There have been many delays."

The woman at the desk held out a slender brown hand. "I shall keep your parcels for you." As Britt hesitated, she added. "Until you return."

"Ah." Britt handed over her bags and followed his elegant back.

"I am Marcel Mariano," he said over his shoulder.

"I shall do my best to play the role of chauffeur." He pointed a key fob at the big green car, then bent and opened the rear door.

Her husband had been indicted for fraud, she had no money, her suitcase was still lost, and she happened to be the one who rated this car. And this chauffeur or whatever he was. She almost fell into the seat. The door closed with a discreet, expensive thump. She had just climbed into a car with a man about whom she knew nothing. A hysterical giggle escaped.

Rules. I'm breaking them faster than they're written.

After the day she'd had, what more could go wrong?

Chapter Eight

Paris

Marcel started the engine, and the car began a quiet, well-mannered purr.

"So, you are not a chauffeur?"

He turned onto a narrow street clogged with traffic. "No." In the mirror, his brow showed no sign of irritation with the cars cutting in and out in front of him. "I am the manager of business for Viane Stephanopolous."

"Viane Stephanopolous?"

"*Oui*. Her legal name is Viane Stephanopolous Thibaudet, but in her work she calls herself Viane Stephanopolous. Today she is filming her podcast, which she hopes to expand into a television show, but there have been many difficulties. The cooking is taking much longer than anticipated. I have been to the market three times to buy more mushrooms. And your friend, Arielle McGregor, must wait until Viane's food preparation is finished. Then she will talk about the wines."

"This is the first show they've done together. Perhaps that makes it more difficult."

His eyes darted to the mirror, and he gazed at her for a moment, brows raised and a slight smile on his lips, as if to say, "Little do you know." Then he said,

"Viane will not tolerate imperfection."

"Arielle says she has a popular restaurant in the town we will visit, Chevalier."

"*Oui*. Viane has, as you Americans say, put Chevalier on the map, but Paris—" He thumped a fist against his chest. "Paris is her heart. She desires to have her own restaurant here. It is her dream."

They rolled slowly along, avoiding pedestrians, bicycles, and darting taxis until he turned onto the sidewalk and stopped facing a tall limestone wall with a wrought iron gate. The gate parted in the middle and swung inward, away from the car. The car glided into a courtyard paved with stone. Marcel stopped again and waited while the gate closed behind them.

"It is the house of the *nonna* of Viane's husband." He crossed himself. "She is now departed."

Directly ahead, a wide stairway ascended to a balcony that ran the width of a three-story limestone mansion. Marble statues of bare-breasted women draped in flowing robes sat on the balcony wall, one at each end and one beside the stair. Half a dozen cats lounged here and there between them, soaking up sunshine.

He turned to the right and parked in front of a smaller building, also constructed of limestone. "The carriage house," he said, as they got out. "It has been remodeled to accommodate Viane's recordings."

He led Britt through a dark green door, down a narrow corridor, and into a warm, dimly-lit room with a large window on one side. Marcel motioned to her to sit on a stool beside the window. "They cannot see us, but we can see them." He pressed a button at the side of the window and a woman's voice, speaking French, came out of a speaker somewhere over Britt's head.

She looked into a kitchen gleaming with copper pots and polished granite countertops. Arielle, elegant in her blue cashmere shift, perched on a stool at one end of the counter. Two cameras appeared to be rolling, the operators with their backs to Britt, one on either side of the stovetop. At center stage, a woman in chef's whites tilted a bowl of morel mushrooms toward one of the cameras. She smiled and chatted at the unblinking electronic eye, then dumped them into a large sauté pan and stirred with a wooden spoon.

She had a round face with a smooth complexion flushed from the heat of the stove, dark eyes, generous red lips, a nicely shaped nose, and thick black hair which she'd tucked under a tall chef's hat. When she smiled, both cheeks dimpled. She was not fat, but in every way round, voluptuous, and beautiful.

Viane added a generous splash of liquor and finished her sauce in a blaze, then poured it over a thick steak that had been grilled and sliced and rested on a bed of greens.

The cameras shifted to follow her as she joined Arielle, who set a basket containing several wine bottles on the counter. She took them out one by one and displayed each label as she described the wine, occasionally asking Viane for help in supplying the correct French word. Finally, each of them raised a glass and said in unison, "*Bon appétit*."

The bright lights went out, and the men behind the cameras rolled them to one side. Viane tore her hat off and threw it in the sink. She yanked out a hair clip and shook free a mass of thick black curls, then pulled the white jacket off and tossed it on the counter. She grabbed a towel and blotted her forehead, throat, and the back of her neck with it.

Marcel opened a door and escorted Britt into the kitchen.

Viane came quickly and grasped both of Britt's hands. "Welcome," she said, with a wide, warm smile. "I am happy to meet Arielle's friend." She kissed Britt's cheeks, one then the other. "Marcel will pour some wine for you, and we can see the video." She pulled another high stool close to the one Arielle had been sitting on. "Please, sit here."

It felt warm and cozy in the kitchen. The cameramen set a large screen on the granite counter and ran cables to it from the back of one of the cameras. One of them handed Viane a remote control. "So you can speed through the parts you don't like," he said with a grin.

"No need. It will be perfect." Marcel lifted his glass of wine. "To Viane and Arielle." As they watched the video, he served hors d'oeuvres of the steak and mushrooms.

The entire day had been totally crazy. Britt couldn't believe she was hungry or that she was sitting there, chatting, eating, and drinking as if nothing was wrong.

After the video ended, Viane jumped up. "I beg you to forgive me. I must hurry." She headed for the door.

"Ladies, *je suis désolé*," Marcel said. "I cannot drive you to the hotel, so I have telephoned for a taxi for you." He followed them down the narrow corridor.

As they went out into the courtyard, he led them to a pedestrian door beside the gate in the stone wall. "I will see you again in Chevalier."

Viane was already halfway up the stair with the statue of the bare-breasted woman at the top. "Marcel, we must prepare," she called. Her voice sounded sharp and anxious. "I do not wish to be late."

Chapter Nine

Paris

Inside the elegant old house, Viane descended the wide, curving staircase, one hand gliding over the gleaming handrail, silver sandals clicking on the marble stairs. This was where she belonged. She was made to live here.

She could barely breathe in the strapless black dress she had bought for this evening. It hugged her body like a second skin—exactly the right thing. If only she could believe spending the evening with a pair of sausage-makers would be worth the effort.

In the spacious foyer by the front door, Marcel Mariano turned sideways to the large, gilt-edged mirror and patted his muscled abs under the burgundy cummerbund. He shrugged into his dinner jacket and surveyed himself again.

"You look perfect, Marcel, as if anything else were possible," Viane said. "For the love of the Holy Mother, will you quit appreciating yourself and get the car? You know I hate to be late."

"The car is waiting."

"Did you engage a driver, then?"

"Of course. Would you prefer that I pretend to be your chauffeur, perhaps?"

She glared at him. "Don't test my patience."

He took the cashmere wrap from her arm and draped it around her bare shoulders. "Do not worry. You are stunning in this dress. Our hosts will be captivated." He held the door, then offered his arm as they walked down the stone steps. "They will, as the Americans like to say, eat out of your hand."

"Ugh! Don't be vulgar." She slid into the car and waited for him to walk around to the other side. "I don't know why I ever thought this would work."

He shrugged his shoulders, lifted his hands, and pushed out his lower lip. "Your husband won't mortgage the farm, and he refuses to touch the money from his grandmother's estate. You can't raise the money yourself. What other chance do you have?"

"That's exactly the problem."

"Remember, it will cost him nothing. It will provide the money you need. And possibly some extra money for him. Simple. You have only to believe it. The *Cochon Qui Rit* will be yours. Repeat that to yourself."

"You don't know Jean-Luc."

"I know he is a man, and like any other man, would prefer to please his wife."

She rolled her eyes. "He would prefer to please God."

"Then tell him he can give his portion of the profit back to God."

"He believes God gave him the ability to create his invention, so he gives the plans away for free."

At the Chez Nous Restaurant, one of the oldest and most expensive in the city, the maître d' escorted them to an intimate corner and a table set with white linen, gleaming silver, and sparkling crystal. The two men, owners of a large sausage-making company in Frankfurt, greeted them with the enthusiasm of cherished friends. They were twins of medium height, gray-eyed, beginning to bald, and dressed in identical black suits and stiff white shirts. They both wore silk bowties, one red, the other blue. "So you can tell us apart," Red Tie said. "I am Gustave Mueller, and my brother is Gunther."

The men refused to talk business while they ate. Instead, they regaled Viane and Marcel with tales of misadventures—each one accompanied by hilarious laughter—they'd had while traveling through South America and Mexico with their wives and assorted small children.

By the time the wine steward presented the third bottle of wine, the knot of dread in Viane's stomach had disappeared. By the time the cheese tray arrived, she had decided Marcel was right. If she promised to donate some of the profits to good works once the restaurant was paid for, surely Jean-Luc would agree.

Over coffee, at last, Gunther and Gustave brought up the contract. "We have stated in our communication with Marcel that in return for the license to manufacture and sell your husband's climate control system we will pay two hundred thousand euros, plus royalties."

It was too good to be true. Viane could barely breathe. With what she had already put down, she would have enough to purchase the *Cochon Qui Rit*.

She pretended nonchalance, as if she made deals like this every day. "We have agreed that it is a fair price."

They handed her a sheaf of papers, then folded their hands. "As you know, we studied various ways to control the temperature and humidity in our sausage facility and concluded that your husband's system is superior to others." They gazed pointedly at her. "However, we have been presented with another, very similar system, at a much lower price. We will honor our offer for forty-eight more hours. If you cannot complete this contract by then, we shall withdraw it."

They were reneging. Viane's world started to spin.

Her smile evaporated the minute they said goodnight. As she stalked out of the restaurant, the long black car Marcel had hired glided to a stop a few feet away. "Those imbeciles. They are nothing more than con men." She slid into the back seat; Marcel followed. "They pretend to be friends, and then they stab a knife in my back." She yanked out the rhinestone-studded clip that held her hair in a French roll, shook her curls free, and rubbed her temples.

Marcel spoke to the driver. "We have had a strenuous evening. Take us to see the lights at the tower. Our nerves require to be soothed." He rolled up the glass screen behind the front seat. "There is still time. You can go to Jean-Luc tomorrow, can you not?"

"I will go. But if I tell him he must sign right away, he will balk."

"We must think of a way to persuade him."

"He never does anything quickly. He always has to ponder. He will pray. He won't make a move unless he is certain it will be pleasing to God."

"Then you must entice him. What might he want that he does not have?"

"Nothing. He is content. He loves his farm. He loves his cows and pigs. He loves to make cheeses and hams and sell them at the markets."

"*Oui*. But there is something he does not have."

"Don't be irritating."

"Children. It is no secret that he would like to have a whole batch of children."

Viane scowled. "Do I look like a breeding sow? Do you think for even one minute that I want to have a bunch of snotty brats clinging to my skirt? Jean-Luc, Jean-Luc, Jean-Luc. How can he be so small, so narrow, so satisfied with himself? Why did I marry such a provincial?"

"Tomorrow you will think of something. Let us put it aside for now. You are tired, and there is nothing more to be accomplished this evening." Marcel opened the console and selected two stemmed glasses, then a bottle of champagne, from which he slowly removed the cork. It hissed softly. "Perfect," he said. "Like the sigh of a nun."

"What do you know about the sigh of a nun?"

"Ah, I have not yet revealed all of my talents to you." He poured a glass and handed it to her. "Give me your feet." He slipped her sandals off, then pulled her feet into his lap and began to rub them. "Drink your champagne."

She *was* tired. Tired of working against the odds. Tired of struggling every day to have enough money. Tired of striving to get something just beyond her reach.

As they passed the iconic tower, Marcel pushed her feet off his lap, leaned toward her, and wrapped a curl of hair around one finger. He tugged gently at the curl until she slid over beside him. It felt good to rest against his warm, athletic body. The car rolled slowly along, rocking her in cushioned comfort.

He put an arm around her and kissed the hollow at the base of her throat. She melted against him, and he swung her up onto his lap, facing him. With both hands, he pushed her skirt up and ran his fingers over her skin, over her lacy garter belt and tights, and after a very long time, as she molded her body to his, he entered the very center of her.

Chapter Ten

Paris

Daylight touched the window, bright enough to shine through the curtains. On the other side of the room, Arielle still snored softly, but Britt had barely slept.

If Rob was convicted of Medicare fraud, then what? He'd go to jail, of course, but what else might happen? As legal owner of Thornton Medical, could she be charged, even though she had nothing to do with running the company? She had checked her phone every hour, hoping to hear from Viktor, but so far, nothing. And now, it was evening in Seattle. Unlikely he'd get back to her. Still, she picked up her phone to check.

A text message popped up, a hand-drawn cartoon. Her sleep-deprived brain struggled to make sense of it, and slowly it dawned on her that she was looking at a caricature of Thirteen's mother. The kid had drawn an unmistakable likeness of her heart-shaped face, shoulder-length hair, and wide, blank, staring eyes.

Britt's mouth went dry, and her hand started to shake. She'd almost forgotten how much she resembled the dead woman. She tapped the information icon at the top of the screen. The sender's phone number did not have a name associated with it. But it couldn't have come from anyone else. The stupid little shit. Thank God she was in Europe. She forwarded it to Oscar. She had enough problems. Let him deal with the juvenile delinquent. She closed the text message, swiped across it, and hit the delete button.

It was a darn good thing she'd been smart enough to put her running gear in her carry-on bag. She pulled on shorts and a tee shirt, slid her feet into her shoes, and a key card into her pocket. As she closed the door, she glanced back at Arielle, still asleep.

No wonder Arielle was tired. Making the video with Viane had kept her on edge all the day before. But from what Britt saw of it, Viane's attention to detail paid off. Both of them had looked great, and hopefully, the podcast would entice viewers to sign up for Arielle's wine tours.

Britt took the stairs down to the lobby and went out into the cool morning air. She began at a brisk walk toward the Eiffel Tower. Then, when she reached the long, green Champs de Mars, she broke into a run. Running always made it easier to think.

Could Rob be guilty of fraud? Whether he was or wasn't, one thing was certain. Life would never be the same again. The only good thing was that her dad wasn't there to watch it happen. Even if Rob were eventually found innocent, a shadow had fallen on Thornton Medical. People who had stayed with the company out of loyalty to her father would probably take their business elsewhere. His life work would dwindle away, and that would haunt her the same way his death did.

What really happened the night her dad vanished into the icy waters of Puget Sound? She had never been able to clarify the circumstances of his death. Neither she nor her mother believed that he committed suicide by jumping off Uncle Brad's boat, but they couldn't disprove it.

That same frustration at her inability to make things right came over her again. It made her want to scream, rip things up, and cry, all at once. She ran harder. Rob had been on board the boat that night, too, and he still insisted he hadn't seen her father disappear. But now she wondered if that was the truth.

Britt shook herself. She needed to shut these thoughts out of her head. They accomplished nothing. Her father was gone. Period. And she was in Paris, dammit, and all she was doing was spoiling the vacation she'd worked so hard for.

Dewdrops sparkled on the grass in the long, wide Champs de Mars park, and at the far end, the enigmatic tower stood, defying time, defying gravity, defying rust and rot and destruction of any kind. It had survived two world wars, and so had many of the people who lived in its shadow. They had endured more heartache and hardship than she ever would.

With a lighter spirit, she ran past the tower and over the bridge across the Seine. Oscar would take care of Thirteen. Viktor would take care of Rob and free up her money. She ran up the stairs to the Trocadero, took a turn around the plaza at the top, and then back down the stairs, back across the river, past the tower, back into the Champs de Mars. Her feet beat steadily on the gravel path. She would get on with building her new life, and although she couldn't quite envision it yet, it would be good.

That's when she saw him. Stan Gibson, the guy

from the FBI, lounging on a bench beside the path, a newspaper in one hand, which he waved at her. She lost her rhythm, stumbled, caught her balance.

"I need to talk to you, okay?" he called.

What could he do to her if she sprinted away? Tempting. She ran all the way to the end of the park. Finally, she turned around and walked back.

"Good morning." He sauntered onto the path that led toward her hotel on rue Cler. "Let's go this way. I'll buy you a *café au lait*."

"You didn't come to buy me coffee." Britt didn't even try to keep the annoyance out of her tone.

"No, but you must admit that it's very civilized of me to do so."

"Look, why don't you just tell me what you want?"

"All right." He stopped. "The missing two-and-a-half million dollars. Do you know where it is?" He watched her face.

"No."

"Do you know anything about it?"

"No." She gazed into his eyes, wondered what might come next.

He walked several paces in silence, then stopped again and turned to face her. "Look at me," he said, and waited until she did. "I saw your reaction yesterday when I told you about the money, so I tend to believe you. But given your expertise in non-verbal communication, if anyone would know how to fake surprise, it would be you."

"I will take that as a compliment."

He held her elbow as they crossed a broad street, dodging morning traffic. Then he paused in front of a café with a broad red and white striped awning that reached out over tidy rows of little round tables. "The fact is, it doesn't matter what *I* think. My colleagues in Seattle believe you have it or know where it is."

"If I had it, do you really think I'd be standing here, talking to you?"

He held up his hand. "Okay. Will you tell me if you think of anything at all that might be pertinent?"

"Of course."

He handed her a card. "My contact information."

She put it in her pocket without looking at it. "I'm thinking I should go home."

"Why would you do that?"

"We need to sell the house. I have to start a new job and buy a condo before school starts in September."

"Ah, you don't understand."

Her heart started to pound. "What now?"

He took her elbow again, steered her to a table under the cheerful awning, and sat down facing the street.

Britt fought down a sense of panic. "*What* don't I understand?"

"Sit."

Her knees went weak. She sank into the chair beside him. A waiter wearing a long white apron appeared at once.

Stan ordered coffee, then gazed earnestly into her eyes. "Look. We have concrete proof that your husband has bilked Medicare out of millions of dollars. Without a shred of doubt, he is going to have to make restitution, and he doesn't have enough to repay even half of it."

"So? What does that mean?"

"It means that the seizure of your assets is neither

partial nor temporary."

"Meaning?"

"You can't sell the house. You can't sell your car, or your husband's car. It's all gone. Everything. Kiss it goodbye."

She pressed a hand over her heart. The noise of the traffic, the bright sunshine, the smells of coffee and fresh bread, everything vanished as she tried to assimilate those words. Finally, she pulled in a breath. "What about my money?"

"Your money is gone."

That couldn't be true. Britt shook her head. "But Viktor di Presti said—"

"Whatever your attorney may have led you to believe, when I say everything, I mean *everything*."

"I earn my own salary. I get royalties from my books. How can you seize that, too?"

"If it was in a joint account, it's gone."

"That can't be right." She hugged her arms to her chest to keep the hollow cavity inside from taking over her whole body. "It's not much, but it's mine. You shouldn't be able to touch it."

"That's not how it works. Believe me, if you know anything at all, it would behoove you to tell me now."

Britt couldn't speak. Her lips trembled. Her eyes stung with tears.

He peered at her. "Your face is white. We'll sit here a bit. Take some deep breaths."

Britt heard the hint of sympathy in his tone. She didn't *want* his sympathy. She leaned her elbows on the table and pressed both hands to her forehead. She drew in one long breath after another, until the world stopped spinning and she could lift her head again.

Stan waited while she sipped a little coffee.

Bad things happened to people all the time, and at least she wasn't dead or dying. Slowly, things came back into focus: the café, the sidewalk bristling with people, and the bicycles and cars darting down the street. She drank some more coffee. Now that she knew the worst, she'd figure it out. She should be grateful that she had her health and Oscar's job offer.

Then he said, "A couple more things."

"Oh, good. It must be my lucky day."

"Actually, the government is suing both your husband and your company, and you own the company. Some of my colleagues argue that, even though you don't run it yourself, you should have known."

It was way too unfair. Her blood started to boil. "That is so lovely. Why don't I just go straight to jail?"

For a nanosecond, his eyes softened and a hint of a smile lifted the corners of his mouth. "Attagirl." Then his face hardened again.

"I can't wait to hear what else you have to say."

He got to his feet and slid some money under the little silver cup holding the bill. "I understand you plan to leave Paris today for Gordes, then go on to Chevalier in a couple of days."

Britt stared up at him. "How do you know that?"

He shrugged. "It's my job to know these things. And my job to intervene if you go astray."

Chapter Eleven

En route to Provence

Moments before the high-speed train from Paris to Avignon started away from the Gare de Lyon, Britt and Arielle settled into their first-class upper-deck seats, facing each other across a little table. Arielle said, "You'll have good connectivity once we're out of the station."

Britt pulled her phone out of her purse. "Looks like I already have."

"Good. Now you can negotiate your salary and start date with Oscar, and then you can relax and enjoy the scenery. In the meantime, the bar car is right next to us. I'll get us some coffee."

To: Oscar Plitman
From: Brittany Ann Thornton
Subject: Analysis of your study on recidivism
Bonjour, Oscar
Since we didn't firm up your job offer before I left, I would like to do so now. Would you reply with the date you expect me to begin work, the length of time you are allotting to the process of analysis and synthesis, and a specific salary?
Thank you so much.
Best regards, Britt
PS: You must have heard by now that Rob has been

indicted for Medicare fraud. What you may not know is that the FBI has seized all of our assets, and it is likely that I will be left with nothing. I will sleep better if I can see the way ahead a little more clearly. B

By the time Arielle returned with two tiny white cups of espresso, Oscar had replied.

To: Brittany Ann Thornton
From: Oscar Plitman
Subject: Analysis of my study on recidivism
Bon nuit, my dear
It's past midnight over here, but since I am still up, I shall answer. I am sorry to tell you that the job is not available. After great deliberation, Martin Sherwood agreed to perform the analysis and write it up. In fact, he has already begun, and he will accompany me to Beijing in September. As you know, his reputation will lend a great deal of gravitas to the results of my work. Oscar

Britt's heart thudded in her chest, and there was that fluttery feeling she got when she was scared. "Read this." She handed her phone to Arielle. "What the f-word am I going to do now?"

Arielle stared at the message. "I think for this, you could go ahead and actually say the f-word. Darn Oscar, anyway. I'm going back to the bar for bloody Marys."

"Better make that a pitcher of them."

To: Oscar Plitman
From: Brittany Ann Thornton
Subject: Analysis of study on recidivism
Oscar,
I believe we had a verbal agreement that I would do the work. Did we not? Britt

She hit "send" and sat back to wait. How was Oscar going to weasel out of this?

To: Brittany Ann Thornton
From: Oscar Plitman
Subject: Analysis of my study on recidivism
My dear,

I'm afraid you let your optimism run away with you, as you are wont to do. We discussed it, and I can see how you misinterpreted our discussion as a verbal agreement. But I did not actually offer you the job.

Enjoy your vacation. You have earned it.

I am certain you will be able to find a position that meets your needs when you return, and if I hear of anything suitable for you, I shall let you know immediately. Oscar

PS: Give my love to the lovely Arielle.

Arielle set a bloody Mary in front of her.

"Bloody Oscar." Britt drank a big gulp. "Please, don't tell me that when God closes one door, he opens another."

Arielle reached across the table and gripped her hand. "This is just plain shitty."

Britt sank back in her seat. "I have to go home."

"Don't say that. Let's think. Who would you talk to about a job? Didn't you say there's going to be an opening at Stanford in the fall?"

"Stanford would be my first choice, but if I wait for that job, I'll be without pay for three or four months, and then I may not get it. There will be a lot of competition from people with more experience. If I were able to go to the International Conference on Deviant Behavior with Oscar, I'd have a good chance, but that's not going to happen."

"All the same, if you want it, then go for it."

"Okay, but even if I knew right now that I would get it, I'd need an interim job."

"Not really. I have plenty of money. We'll share, and you can pay me back whenever."

Britt shook her head. This day was just as crazy as the day before. "I can't do that. But thanks."

"But look. Everything is online, so you can do a job search from here. Besides, you might have to interview in Boston or Miami or San Francisco. Or somewhere in between. You can go from Paris as easily as you can from Seattle." Arielle grinned. "Think about it. And drink up. I have a totally brilliant idea."

Chapter Twelve

Chevalier

Jean-Luc Thibaudet stood beside the large round stainless tank, stirring the milk with the long wooden paddle, watching it swirl in lazy circles. Jacqueline slipped into the cheese-making room. She took a clean white jacket from the shelf beside the old wood door, buttoned it on over her school uniform, and then took the thermometer from the cupboard. She came to stand beside him and immersed the thermometer. "Papa, is Viane coming back today?"

Jean-Luc's hands hesitated a moment, then resumed stirring. "*Oui, ma petite.* She will be here very soon."

Jacqueline removed the thermometer and held it up so he could read it.

He nodded. "It is good."

"Papa, it wasn't nice what Viane said about me the night before she went to Paris."

"Pay no attention. She was not angry with you. She was angry with me."

"Papa!" Her voice rose, and Jacqueline eyed him with intense concentration. "Don't pretend. It means she does not *like* me."

"*Ma Petite*, listen. When Viane is angry, she says things she does not mean. Everyone does so. Even me.

64

Even you. You are soon to have eleven years. That is old enough to know that married people do not always agree. They do not always want the same thing. How would that be possible? It is not. Two different people will always have different ideas."

Jacqueline's brow puckered in a worried frown. "Viane wants to live in Paris. We will not go to live in Paris, will we Papa?"

"*Non, non.* I do not wish to live anywhere but here."

"You could get a divorce. You could, you know. Then you could marry someone who likes to be here with us."

"*Ma petite*, it is wrong to take marriage vows so lightly."

****

Jean-Luc left his boots at the door and went into the kitchen. He loved the big heart of the old stone farmhouse. Viane had insisted on installing new appliances and repainting everything, but otherwise he had persuaded her to keep it the same as it had always been, an open space where the family lived. Whether they were reading in a chair by the hearth, eating at the round oak table, or cooking, they were together.

It warmed his heart to see Jacqueline sitting at the table, her head bent over her mathematics workbook. He set a basket of new baby potatoes on the counter beside the sink and pulled a handful of spring peas out of his shirt pockets. "Look, the beginnings of a lovely fresh vegetable soup."

Jacqueline lifted her head and smiled.

Just as he filled a pan with water to wash the potatoes, Viane's forest green sedan swept up the drive.

Moments later, the entry door closed with a thump and her heels clicked on the stone floor in the foyer where they hung their coats. She bustled into the kitchen, accompanied by the scent of jasmine and carrying a large basket. She gave a brittle little burst of laughter. "My dear, look how domestic you've become." She set the basket on the counter beside him and stood on tiptoes to kiss his cheek. "And Jacqueline," she said in her high-pitched, sing-song, talking-to-a-child voice, "so busy."

He hadn't realized it before, but she always talked to her that way.

"Hello, Viane." Jacqueline folded her books together and walked toward the hallway. "I will study in my room, Papa."

Jean-Luc stood still for a moment, looking from one to the other.

Viane waggled her fingers as if waving goodbye. "Don't work too hard." Her voice was too cheery, too bright.

As long as he could remember, the house had felt safe and comfortable. Even when his parents quarreled, which had, at times, seemed often, it felt good to be together. But now, it buzzed with uncomfortable energy. This energy had arrived with Viane. Like a storm, it followed her in the door. It grew while she pushed aside his new potatoes and peas and replaced them with sorrel and salmon she'd brought from Paris.

He went to the barn to check on the cows while she cooked. Then he went to the cellars and looked in on the hams and cheeses. But when he came back into the house, the air still felt charged. He told himself he was being fanciful.

While they ate the excellent meal she prepared, he wished Jacqueline would engage in conversation with Viane, but she kept her eyes on her plate and responded only when spoken to. She cleared the dishes and stacked them in the dishwasher with none of her usual chatter.

Normally, he would sit in the old leather chair by the fire after dinner and read the newspaper; Jacqueline would finish her homework at the table. He would glance up occasionally to ask how she was getting on and be rewarded with a smile, but this night, she went back to her bedroom.

As soon as he sat down, Viane brought him a sheaf of papers. "Please read this, my dear. As I said on the telephone, I have found a way to buy the restaurant and at the same time, provide more income for you, all without mortgaging the farm or touching a penny of your grandmother's money." She flashed a wide smile as she settled on the arm of his chair.

He glanced at the header on the first page, read the first paragraph, and then looked up at her. "A contract to license my climate control system?"

"*Oui*. It is a very good contract, but we must act quickly."

"If these men need a system to keep their sausages at a constant temperature and humidity, they only need to telephone, and I will tell them how to do it."

"But they want to manufacture it and sell it."

"I see that." He shook his head. "You have talked about selling my invention before. I did not wish to do so then, and I do not wish to do it now." He laid the papers on the floor beside his chair.

"This is different. You would still own the patent.

The license would simply allow them to use it."

"Yes, and they would make everyone pay for something God freely gave to me."

She stalked back and forth in front of him. "After the restaurant is paid for, it will provide an additional income stream for us. You won't be so dependent on the farm, on your hard work. And it will cost you nothing. Nothing!"

"I have benefited from the help of many people. Why wouldn't I help others? What kind of person would I be to sell it for money?"

"It is not a sin to make money. Your name will become well known. It will increase the demand for your cheeses and hams."

"Already, people come from all around to buy them at the market."

"They will command top prices."

"My prices are fair. I would not change that."

"Why are you so obstinate about this?" She stalked to the kitchen counter, poured a glass of wine, and took a long drink. "Don't you understand that I am thinking of you?"

"No." He shook his head. "You are thinking of yourself." He had admired her fiery spirit when they first married, but now he knew it came from the deep well of discontent that resided in her soul. "Listen, Viane. Having more, having this restaurant in Paris will not make you happy. What will make you happy is to think how good the life you have is."

She stalked back and forth, her petite form vibrating with anger. "I have invested all my own money to secure the option to buy the *Cochon Qui Rit*. It has two stars already. It is my dream to bring it up to three stars. I know I can do this. But I need your help."

"This sounds very much like what you told me when you wanted the brasserie here in Chevalier. You thought that would make you happy, but it did not. Now you want this, but it will not make you happy either. And you would be away from home even more.

"If you would let the work and the days flow as they have for thousands of years already, if you would find joy in the rising of the sun and the changing of the seasons, if you would know that you are in the best place on earth, then you would need nothing more. Instead, you make yourself discontented."

She poured a second glass of wine and brought it to him, then sat on the arm of his chair.

He gazed at the wine for a moment but did not drink. "If you follow this path, you will always want more. You will never feel satisfied. Alternatively, you could discover how to be content with what you have. It is possible for you to do this."

After a moment, she put her arm around his shoulders. "I should have waited. You are tired after working so hard all day. It will be different in the morning."

He shifted away, to the far side of the chair, away from the scent of her skin, warm and musky. He watched her push that cloud of black curls away from her face, revealing the curve of her cheek and her perfect little nose. He knew she expected to feel his hand on her back now, and then she would slip down onto his lap. But after, when she lay beside him in the bed, she would tell him again that he must sell the gift God had given him.

Chapter Thirteen

Chevalier

Inspector Édouard Guillaume Chevalier awoke early, at the first sound of the doves under the olive trees. It was market day. More than that, today Viane would make her video, and an exceptional number of people would converge on the town square to watch.

She would walk through the market with the American woman and talk about the vegetables, the olives, the cheese, and the charcuterie that had made their market famous. The video would be a success, he knew.

Viane had always insisted that everything be perfect. Even when they played together after school, her clothes must never be soiled, her hair must always be held just so in her barrettes, and he must keep his shirt tucked in if he would spend the afternoon with her.

When she went to Paris to study chemistry at the Sorbonne, he waited for her, but she returned and married Jean-Luc. And broke his heart. Édouard inspected himself in the mirror. The creases in his trousers looked knife-blade sharp, his shirt crisp and fresh. Too skinny, his mother always said, and admonished him to eat, but he did eat. It was his fate to be as long and thin as a zipper. His hair stuck up all over his head, making him look startled, as if the prematurely white color were not startling enough. He smoothed it down with hands full of gel, and at last satisfied that it would stay that way, put on round, black-framed glasses. He paused in the kitchen long enough to brew an espresso, then drove to work.

He parked beside the stream that marked the edge of the town, near the huge old willow, and walked up the hill into Chevalier, the village named for his great-great grandfather, the place he belonged, where he wished to spend his life. He marched through the market square at the top, then past Viane's brasserie. Farther up the hill, at the car park, he opened the gate and pulled the sign with the large letter P into the street, where it would be clearly visible.

****

Britt propelled Arielle's little red sportscar toward Chevalier, occasionally glancing over at Arielle, who sat in the passenger seat, frowning, scribbling in a little notepad, and frowning some more. Clearly, she felt unprepared for the morning ahead.

The cool, sweet air ruffled her hair. The valley, hushed, barely awake, lay in deep shadow, its colors bold and rich, vibrant. At every turn of the narrow road, a new delight unfolded. Long sloping fields of red poppies, cherry boughs reaching over the road and drooping under the weight of their fruit, a weathered stone farmhouse with an old blue tractor idling in the yard and fluffy brown chickens pecking at the ground around it.

The night before, her mother had assured her that Megan had slipped right into her summer routine in California, swimming and going to the beach with the boy next door, just as she did every year. It was such good news that it started a song in her heart. Now she could believe that everything would work out, in spite of the fact that Megan's text messages were generally snarky and undoubtedly sent only at her grandmother's insistence.

So what if she was getting divorce? So what if she had no money and no job? Megan was healthy and happy, and her attorney, Viktor di Presti, had assured her that she, personally, would not be charged with fraud. Okay, so he was a lawyer, right? So, he would never say anything for absolutely sure, but she could tell that's what he meant. She had much to be grateful for, right?

She guided the car around another curve and caught her breath. High above the valley, sunlight shimmered on Chevalier's pale gold limestone walls. Hewn from the rock on which it stood, the village glowed like a jeweled crown. No wonder Arielle raved about it.

They crossed a bridge over a sparkling stream at the foot of the hill. The road funneled down to one lane, and almost at once, they were in the town. The car rumbled up a steep, narrow cobblestone street between two- and three-story buildings. On both sides, almost close enough to reach out and touch, geraniums spilled out of window boxes below weathered wood shutters.

Arielle held up her watch. "Omigod, we're late. Viane is going to have a cow!" She sighed. "What I won't do to promote my business. If I live through this, please, please, please have a glass of champagne ready when I'm done."

"Breathe." Britt lifted an eyebrow. "And tell me again why you want to live here, where Queen Viane holds court and everyone bows down."

Arielle grinned. "You'll see. It's perfect, especially if I can buy the cheese shop. You know I've always wanted to own one. And Viane's brasserie has put the place on the map, so lots of tourists visit."

"All potential customers for your wine tours."

"Exactly."

"Just keep telling yourself that."

Arielle blew out a breath. "I'll be fine as soon as we finish this darn video." The car came to a semi-flat opening, which Arielle identified as the town square. It was not large, about a third of a city block in size, and more like a pentagon than a square, but it did have a fountain in the middle and big stone buildings with doors opening into shops and cafés on every side. Arielle pointed to the right. "Drop me at her restaurant, and I'll go face Medusa."

Viane's restaurant anchored the highest part of the square. It had a terrace which floated several feet above the street like a stage. On it, a cluster of tables waited, each with a dark green umbrella, unfurled and pointing to the sky, where a few wispy clouds gleamed against the brilliant blue of the immeasurable universe. Britt stopped at the bottom of a stairway leading to the door.

Arielle climbed out. "Don't forget. Champagne."

"Got it. Now go break a leg."

A block away, up an even steeper grade, a tall, thin officer pulled a sign with a large letter P into place at the edge of the street. His uniform shirt, crisply starched, lay flat across his belly. His pants sported sharp creases. Britt headed up the hill as he walked down. He touched his hat and nodded as she passed.

She parked and followed the officer back down to

the square. She stood for a minute and looked around, wondering which store might be the cheese shop Arielle hoped to buy.

Arielle could easily pay for it, so that was not a problem. But would she feel at home here? Would she be able to put down roots, manage both her wine-tour business and a shop, and thrive? No wonder she wanted Britt to stay and help. That was a lot for one person to accomplish on her own, even someone as energetic and optimistic as Arielle. After all, she was an outsider in a country where the second language was wine and cheese.

Across the square, sunlight warmed the faded blue awning above the door of a café and pulled Britt along in its beam. She settled into a chair at an outside table and placed her market basket beside her feet. For the first time since Stan Gibson had dropped his little bombshell on her, she was actually enjoying being in France. It was weird, really. First the FBI took everything she owned. Then Oscar gave the job she wanted to Martin Sherwood. She had nothing more to lose. Zero. Nada. Zip. And instead of feeling anxious, she felt free, even giddy at times, as if seeing the world with new eyes.

Very weird. She still had to take care of Megan, and she did have to get a job, so how could she be free? It made no sense, but that was how she felt.

Near the fountain in the middle of the square, a man with a wide-brimmed leather hat opened the side door of a red van and started unloading, first, a large round table, then a big green umbrella, which he positioned over the table.

Her stomach rumbled, and as if on cue, a short man

with wiry black hair and warm brown eyes appeared at her little table. His bright white apron and shirt were so stiff they crackled. After the required exchange of greetings, she ordered a *petit déjeuner.*

Vendors were setting up their stalls and giant umbrellas to shade them. The first man paused frequently to call out a greeting. He placed a large wood cutting block beside a heavy old scale and sharpened a knife with a long, curving blade, drawing it across a stone in even strokes that rang in the air. The freshly scoured metal glinted in the sun, which now bathed the entire square in clear yellow light.

Britt liked the way he moved about. He looked calm, comfortable with his task, comfortable with his neighbors, comfortable in his own skin. From the back of the truck, he brought out a huge wheel of cheese, a giant ham, strings of sausages, and smaller cheeses. Before driving off, he covered his wares with a spotless white cloth.

Britt pulled her journal out of the market basket at her feet and began to sketch the table in the center of the square. She drew the ham, cheeses, strings of sausages, and then a man of medium height with a square, sturdy chest and wearing a broad-brimmed hat. The pencil hovered over his face. A strong face, rectangular jaw. Wide eyes under dark, slightly bushy brows. Eyes that seemed to see everything. A nose. A nice nose. A moustache, yes, curving down and then up as it tapered away from full lips. Lips that would be nice to kiss. She laid the pencil on the table and slid her fingertips over the page. He felt solid, earthy, magnetic.

The scent of cigar smoke told her she wasn't alone. A thick brown finger rested on her sketch. "It's not right." A pleasant baritone voice. "The nose *doit être*— it must be more long, and with a bump in it."

The man with the leather hat stood beside her, so close to her shoulder that she sensed the heat of his body. He smelled of herbs and sunshine and a good cigar. Her skin prickled with longing to be touched. Britt sucked in a breath. If she didn't get a little space, she couldn't be responsible for what she might do. She gestured with an open palm at the other chair beside the little round table.

"*Merci*," he replied, and sat. "For *un moment*, while you fix my nose." He looked solemn, the way a man looks when he stands in front of the preacher, about to say, "I do."

Britt picked up her pencil. She hesitated, then handed it to him. His hand brushed hers as he took it. She felt the color rise in her cheeks, felt the tempo of her heart kick up a notch, held her breath as she watched him redraw his nose with a couple of quick lines.

He smiled. "Madame, your breakfast is arriving. *Bon appétit*." He stood, touched the brim of his hat, and walked away.

The waiter stood beside her. "Ah, *bien*," he said. "You have drawn Jean-Luc."

"Jean-Luc?" Britt asked.

"You do not know this man?" the waiter asked.

Britt shook her head.

"But you have drawn him perfectly." In front of her, he placed a tray with little ceramic pots of butter and jam, two short, silver pitchers, and a basket containing a croissant and a piece of long, thin baguette sliced lengthwise.

"You know him?"

"*Oui. Certainement.* Everyone knows him. He is a good man."

Jean-Luc. Britt stared at the sketch, then looked up at Jean-Luc, who was tying a starched white apron around his solid, comfortable-sized waist, wrapping the long narrow ties completely around and knotting them in front. The contrasting white made his forest-green shirt stand out, crisp and handsome. A good man. He bent to speak to a diminutive old woman wearing a heavy sweater and carrying a huge basket of flowers on her back. He placed a hand on the woman's shoulder and bent farther so she could kiss his cheek, and then a truck lumbered past and hid him.

Britt poured steaming coffee from one silver pitcher and hot milk from the other and began to eat. When she looked up again, women with baskets and elderly ladies with sensible shoes and two-wheeled carts had begun to circle the stalls, selecting tomatoes, asparagus, and bunches of pale green endive.

A flock of men and women dressed in black flitted around Jean-Luc's stall. Beside it, they set up a patio-type table made of wrought iron, and two matching chairs. One placed a yellow-and-blue cloth on the table, then a vase of yellow flowers and several bottles of wine. Others laid out power cords and an array of lights. Obviously, they were part of the film crew.

The plan was that Viane would talk about dishes made from ingredients in the market, and then, while her husband sampled the food, Arielle would discuss wine pairing. It looked as if the activity would center on the table with the blue and yellow cloth, right beside Jean-Luc's market table with the cheeses and hams.

And the crew was talking to him and gesturing. So, he had to be Viane's husband. A little pang of regret sneaked into Britt's heart. She hurried to squash it. She told herself they would make a handsome couple.

Across the square, the door to the restaurant opened. Three men balancing cameras on their shoulders came out, then Marcel, tall and elegant, then Viane in chef's whites, then Arielle in her pink blouse. She stood stiffly erect, a sign that she was a tiny bit anxious.

Viane and Arielle, each with a basket in hand, came down the steps from the terrace. The camera operators walked backward, filming as the women chatted with vendors and filled their baskets with produce. Marcel, looking graceful and composed in his gray silk shirt, cleared the way. A dozen schoolgirls about ten years old, all wearing plaid skirts and white blouses, followed with their teacher.

Carrot tops and parsley drooped artistically over the rim of their baskets when they finally came to Jean-Luc's table. Chatting and looking into the camera, Viane held up wedges of cheese, and then they both tasted slices of ham, offered on the tip of his long, curved knife.

A man wearing a chef's jacket and hat came from the restaurant and placed a quiche, a bowl of salad, and a baguette beside the flowers on the blue and yellow tablecloth. Viane showed the quiche, then cut a slice and placed it on a plate in front of Jean-Luc, who had seated himself. He took a couple of bites, gave it a thumbs up, and nodded.

Arielle poured a glass of wine. Finally looking at ease, she held the rosy-pink color in front of the camera, then set it in front of Jean-Luc. She picked up a second bottle and displayed the label, then began to open it.

The cameras focused on Viane again as she tossed the salad. She scooped up a plateful, garnished it with round red chili peppers, and placed it in front of her husband. He wiped his moustache on a large white napkin and popped a pepper in his mouth. Then another.

Arielle opened a third bottle of wine, white this time, and filled another glass. Viane took the glass, sipped, and turned back to face the cameras.

Out of the corner of her eye, Britt saw Jean-Luc's face turn red, then purple. His chair grated on the cobblestones, and he lurched to his feet.

There was a collective gasp from the crowd. Behind the cameramen, one of the girls broke away from her classmates and teacher. "Papa!" She rushed toward him.

His breath rasped in his throat.

Britt could hear it fifty feet away. She jumped up. He fell forward, his head and chest crashing down onto the quiche and salad. Britt sprinted toward him. In slow motion, he began to slide backward off the table, pulling the cloth, the food, and the wine bucket with him. His knees hit the ground, then his hips.

The girl grabbed his arm, as if to lift him up. "Papa!" she screamed.

Britt swooped down and caught his head just in time to keep it from hitting the pavement. His face was purple, his neck veins distended, his dark brown eyes full of fear. They looked into hers for a long moment, then fluttered and closed.

She lifted his jaw to check his airway. She bent over him, her ear to his nose, her eyes watching his chest. Nothing. "He's not breathing." Britt heard her own voice as if from a far distance. It sounded strong and sure. As if she weren't terrified that this lovely man might die. "Arielle," she yelled, "call 911."

The teacher crowded in beside her, an epinephrine pen in her hand. Viane grabbed the teacher's shoulder. "No, no, he's not allergic to anything. Don't waste your medication. You may need it." But the teacher jabbed it into him anyway. Then she got to her feet and wrapped her arms around the crying girl.

The police officer Britt had seen earlier knelt opposite her. He pressed his fingertips to Jean-Luc's neck, searching for a pulse. "His heart is still beating," he said, close to her ear and quiet. "Is he choking?"

She tilted Jean-Luc's head back farther and peered into his mouth. "Nothing visible." She sealed her lips over his and blew. His chest rose. "He's not choking. His airway is open, but he's not breathing." Again, she sealed his lips with her own, and blew. Again, his chest rose.

The officer still had his fingers on Jean-Luc's neck. "His heart just stopped."

She yanked the dark green shirt open, sending buttons, a small red pepper, and bits of lettuce and quiche flying. The officer placed his hands over his heart and began to pump.

The world coned down to this one tiny spot where she knelt, willing blood to flow through his arteries and veins, trusting that he had enough oxygen in his system to sustain him, hoping for a sign, a cough, a flutter of the eyelids, anything that showed a return to this world.

Sounds muted. Her vision blurred. Her heart raced. She blew air into his lungs every time the officer stopped chest compressions to check for a pulse. She knew that chest compressions alone were supposed to be sufficient, but he was so still. She had to do *something*. She watched his color fade to gray, felt his life slipping away, prayed for help, prayed for a miracle.

Medics arrived. Britt felt Arielle's hands on her shoulders, urging her to her feet, pulling her back to allow the medics room. Arielle helped her sit on the stone ledge that encircled the fountain, then sat down beside her. "Hold on," Arielle said. Her voice sounded far away. "You okay?"

The medics administered a shot right into Jean-Luc's neck and fought to pass a tube into his lungs. Britt willed them to start his heart, to send breath back into his body. At last, they lifted him onto the stretcher and moments later, the ambulance rolled away.

Viane stood watching the ambulance, frowning, her eyes staring, her lips pressed together.

All Britt's instincts were buzzing. She shivered. "She's his wife."

"Yes," Arielle replied.

"She is displeased—angry even."

"Certainly not. I'm sure she's scared."

"She should look scared, but she doesn't."

"You've spent too much time with Oscar, studying madmen and criminals."

Chapter Fourteen

Chevalier

Britt watched the big green sedan slip through the crowd, Marcel driving, Viane sitting beside him. It disappeared down the narrow, cobbled road.

The girls in school uniforms circled the one who was crying. They put their arms around each other, and the teacher hugged them all. Gradually, shoppers began to move around Britt and Arielle. They bought almonds and olives, parsley and radishes. Voices took up conversations that had lapsed while Jean-Luc lay on the ground.

The officer and a woman with auburn hair, whom he called Monique, carried Jean-Luc's cheeses and hams into the store next to the café where Britt had eaten breakfast. The men and women dressed in black rolled up power cords and took the lights away. They carried the food, the wine, and the wrought-iron table to Viane's restaurant. They helped the officer fold up Jean-Luc's umbrella, then carried that away too. In a few minutes, there was no sign he'd even been there.

Arielle brought a glass of water. "You look pale."

Britt lifted the glass to her lips, but the water spilled down the front of her chic Paris dress. She touched her fingertips to her mouth.

Arielle frowned. "What's wrong?"

"My lips are numb. There's an acrid taste in my mouth. I feel like puking, and I'm dizzy."

"I don't want *you* to have a heart attack too. Let's get you out of the sun."

Britt got to her feet, swayed, clung to her friend.

Arielle linked their arms together. "Come on, you must have left your purse at the café."

As they walked through the ring of vendor stalls, Britt stopped. She turned to look at the empty hole in the middle. Jean-Luc should be there, carving off slices of ham and offering samples on the tip of his long, sharp knife. She wished she believed in praying.

The outdoor tables at the café where she'd eaten breakfast were full. "But *attendez*," the waiter said, "*un petit moment*." He disappeared into the café and returned with her basket. "I kept it for you." He gazed at her face, then gestured toward the door. "I have a small table inside, if you would rest here."

As he held her chair, he said, "You were *magnifique*. So quick to help Jean-Luc. Everyone says what a blessing Viane is to our village. And it is true. But also Jean-Luc. I pray to the saints for him." He crossed himself. "*S'il vous plaît*, may I bring you something?"

Britt felt desperate for caffeine. "Coffee, please."

He brought it quickly, and after a few sips, her head started to clear. "Arielle, it's very strange. He stopped breathing before his heart stopped, and respiratory arrest is rare in a healthy adult."

"The teacher emptied an epinephrine pen into him. Could it have been anaphylactic shock?"

"But why would Viane give him something that he's allergic to?"

"She didn't cook the quiche herself."

Britt frowned. "How can we find out how he's doing?"

"Édouard will know."

"Édouard?"

"Édouard Chevalier, the police officer."

"Chevalier? Like the name of the town?"

"Yes. His great-great grandfather, or somebody like that was the founding father." Arielle squinted at Britt's face. "You look like you're feeling better."

"I'm okay." She still felt nauseous, but her lips were no longer numb, and her dizziness had subsided.

"If you're sure, why don't you sit here a while? I'll go see if we can check in to the B&B."

"Good idea." Something was wrong. Something didn't make sense. Britt searched for a logical explanation for Jean-Luc's symptoms, but it was like putting together a jigsaw puzzle with pieces that didn't belong.

Arielle hesitated. "Maybe you can lie down while I talk to Monique about buying her cheese shop."

How could she think with Arielle fussing around? "Quit hovering. Go. I'll be fine."

****

As Viane and Marcel approached the hospital, Marcel broke the silence. "Shall I assume that you signed a marriage pact before the wedding?"

"What do you expect? His parents insisted that we have a contract, and he always did what they told him." She stared out the window. "They forced me. I had to agree to a complete separation of property."

Jean-Luc's mother, that old cow, had swallowed a bitter pill the day her precious son got married. You'd have thought Viane had come to steal the silver. She ruled the family the same as always, and Jean-Luc, of course, complied.

"But he gave you the brasserie in your own name, *n'est-ce pas*?"

"*Oui*."

"That was a very generous gift."

Viane glared at Marcel. "Everything else is his, his alone, to do as he wishes."

"If he dies?"

She pursed her lips and looked out the window.

"I assume there's a will and let me guess—you are the beneficiary."

"I am."

Marcel shot her a look. "The farm, the house in Paris, his inheritance, all of it will be yours?"

"Don't be tedious, Marcel."

"How nice. I also assume that you will become responsible for Jacqueline. You will become her adoring mother."

Chapter Fifteen

Chevalier

Édouard looked around the square, hoping to spot the woman who had helped Jean-Luc. Her hair and dress said Paris, but she spoke with an American accent. He went to the café, where she had been sitting earlier, stepped inside, and saw her at once. She looked exhausted. But, of course, it had been a shock.

"Madame," he said with a little bow, "permit me to introduce myself. I am Inspector Édouard Chevalier."

"Brittany Thornton." She shook his hand, then gestured toward the other chair, inviting him to sit across from her at the tiny round table. "Have you heard anything?"

"*Oui*, I came to tell you. Jean-Luc reached the hospital and is responding to treatment, although it is not certain that he will live."

She leaned toward him over the checkered red and white cloth, her eyebrows pinched together in concern, and spoke very quietly. "What do you think caused him to stop breathing?" Her eyes watched his face, alert, intent, intelligent.

"I don't know," he replied. "I expect that the doctor will tell us."

"He seemed strong and healthy. Is he not?"

Édouard shook his head. "Jean-Luc is never ill, not

even for a day."

"Does he have an illness or a severe allergy?"

"I believe I would know if he did, but I know of nothing."

She spoke so softly he could barely hear her. "I met Viane a few days ago in Paris, and I have heard that she wants very much to buy a restaurant there. I have also heard that she would need her husband's help to buy it, but he has refused." Again, she gazed earnestly at him.

He waited. Obviously, she had more to say.

"I am a psychologist, with a specialty in abnormal psychology, so I think of things differently than most people. And I wonder, is she so determined to have this restaurant that she would harm her husband?"

His back jerked up straight. "No. Surely not. I have known her all my life. No. You must not think such a thing."

He took a deep breath, ready to explain, then hesitated. This woman could never understand Viane as he did. No one could. Explain how she hates to be remembered as the poor girl, the child of an abusive, alcoholic father. Explain how, for years, she was unwelcome in certain homes. Explain how she is driven. But he stopped himself. Because if he told this woman with the discerning eyes, Viane would seem to be ruthless.

He shook his head. This had gone far enough. "Madame," he said firmly, "I am certain there is a simple reason for Jean-Luc's illness. Soon the doctor will have his diagnosis, a clear, reasonable explanation. I shall ask him what that is." *And this preposterous notion will be shown to be false.* "You must not allow your imagination to harm an innocent person."

She sat back for a moment, then asked, "How long has Jean-Luc been married to Viane?"

Édouard bit back a sharp rebuke. This Brittany Thornton was a stranger, a stranger who had no right to cast aspersions. Still, she had been good to help Jean-Luc, so he would be kind. "Four years. Perhaps five." He knew exactly when Viane had walked down the aisle but felt compelled to conceal this information.

She looked away, as if searching for something. "Is it a happy marriage?" she asked finally, watching him.

This morning, Viane looked ravishing, her cheeks full of color, her black hair and red lips outstanding against the white chef's jacket. He had never seen her look more beautiful. But had she reached out for Jean-Luc? Had she called out his name? He thought not.

The earth shifted under his feet. He slumped in his chair. "Is it a happy marriage?" he repeated softly. He had believed all the time while Viane was in Paris at the Sorbonne, earning her degree in chemistry, that she would come back to Chevalier, and then he would ask her to be his wife, and she would say yes. Her marriage to Jean-Luc had grieved him, broken his heart. And he had continued to long for her.

But now, he knew. Living with Viane would be tumultuous. If he were her husband, he would be constantly striving to give her what she wanted, what she needed, to make her happy. And failing. And his beloved old farmhouse—Viane would hate to live in such an ancient, drafty pile of stone.

It was as if Madame Thornton had snapped her fingers and awakened him from a trance. "Is it a happy marriage?" he said again. "I don't know." Nonetheless, he did know. How could her marriage be happy when

Viane was never happy?

But he couldn't tell this woman with the disquieting gaze. "Why do you ask?" He sat forward again and peered into her eyes.

For the first time, she looked away. "He is a man who should have a happy marriage."

Édouard recalled how she had pressed her cheek to Jean-Luc's chest, tipped back his head to see if he could breathe. The fear was plain on her face when she looked at him and said, "No breath."

He said, "How is it that you know Jean-Luc?"

She smiled and gave a slight shrug. She looked...wistful. "I don't, not really. I only spoke with him for a few minutes before the market this morning, here at the café."

Édouard sighed. What a mystery it was, that Jean-Luc so quickly inspired her to care about him. Only Monique had ever had such a look for him.

Again, the earth shifted. When had he fallen out of love with Viane? When had he started to love Monique, the woman whose sensibilities so closely matched his own? He jumped up. "Please excuse me."

Chapter Sixteen

Chevalier

Britt watched Chevalier go. In his haste, he banged against a chair, knocked it over, and dashed out without stopping to right it. How odd!

For several minutes, she sat quietly, barely aware of the hum of conversation all around her. Jean-Luc's airway wasn't blocked, so how come he stopped breathing? She opened her journal and ran her fingers lightly over her sketch, as if it might tell her something.

In her experience, respiratory arrest in an otherwise healthy adult happened when someone overdosed on opioids. But she felt pretty sure that narcotics wasn't it. She picked up her phone to search for other potential causes of his symptoms.

Just then, Arielle came in, hobbling as fast as she could—something she never did—a giant grin on her face, her cheeks flushed, her gray-blue eyes sparkling.

Britt jumped up and hugged her. "It's all over you. Monique agreed to sell you the cheese shop."

"Yes, and there's an apartment on the floor above that goes with it, and a storeroom behind the shop where they hid people from the Nazis in World War II. I can clean it up and move my office in; everything I need in one place."

"I bet Allistair is dancing in heaven."

"I know. It's exactly what he wanted—what we both wanted." Her eyes misted over. "I only wish he were here." She sighed, and then her voice became business-like again. "She wants to close the deal immediately."

"Immediately?"

"Since I have cash, as soon as she gets the money, like, tomorrow. She's eager to move to Roussillon, but will live with her grandmother for a little while and teach me to run the shop. The problem is those wine tours I've booked in the next couple of weeks."

"I could stay here. That was your brilliant idea, right, that I'd work for you, and you'd pay the rent on a condo for me when I go home?"

"But I didn't expect you to start so soon. I thought it would take a while to finalize the purchase. I thought you'd have time to go to Bordeaux and Champagne with me first."

Britt waved a hand. "I'll go another time." The truth was, the very idea of pretending she could taste the terroir in a thimbleful of wine—not to mention driving around in a minibus and making small talk with a bunch of tourists—while Jean-Luc's life hung on a thread made her crazy.

"Do you really want to take on the management of the shop?"

"Sure. I know how to cut cheese in English. French cheese—I dunno, but I bet I can do it."

"I feel like I'm taking advantage of you. I'll be happy to pay a couple more months' rent, but I'm still going to owe you big time."

Britt laughed. "And I don't owe you?"

Arielle squinted at her. "You're just saying that."

"Please. I'm happy to do it. And it's a big relief to have the rent taken care of when I get home."

"Then I'll go to the bank to arrange the transfer of funds. But first" —Arielle gestured toward the door— "let's check in at the B&B. It's right across the square and belongs, incidentally, to Monique's grandparents."

Half an hour later, Britt closed the door to her room in the B&B.

She plunked her suitcase on the stand, pulled out her laptop, and plugged it in. Sitting cross-legged on the bed with its cheerful yellow-hibiscus comforter, she waited impatiently for her browser to open.

Besides opioids, there must be other causes of respiratory arrest. There were weird genetic conditions, of course, but that wouldn't explain the bitter taste in her mouth or the numbness of her lips. Plus, she'd felt weak, confused, and dizzy. Poison was the only thing she could think of. Arielle would say that was because she spent too much time studying psychopaths, and she could be right. Or not.

Perhaps someone had slipped a poisonous mushroom into the quiche or salad. That happened, not always accidentally, more often than most people thought. So, who might have had the motive, means, and opportunity? Well, du-uh. His wife, obviously. Probably others as well, even though he seemed well-liked, but definitely Viane.

Huh. Poisoning someone in plain sight, right in front of a whole group of people. Gutsy. But what a great idea!

Britt sucked in a deep breath. Her instincts told her she was on the right path, but the little voice in the back of her brain, which sounded remarkably like Oscar

Plitman, reminded her that her instincts were unreliable. Just like her instincts about Thirteen. They proved nothing. She needed facts.

Her fingers danced on the keyboard: "poison respiratory arrest death." Pages upon pages of links flooded the screen. She scowled at it. It would take forever and a day to work through all that.

Time to go for a run, to let her subconscious work on the problem. She found her running shoes and put them on. Once outside, her legs still felt weak, so she walked, wending her way down a steep, narrow, cobblestone street between old stone buildings with pots of geraniums on every stairway. After a few minutes, she came to the stream she had driven across that morning, the dividing line between the town and the valley with its orchards and fields of poppies. Beside the bridge, a huge willow draped over the water.

Vaguely aware that her phone had been vibrating, she pulled it out of her pocket. A cartoon splashed onto the screen. She stared at it, trying to make it okay, trying to make it look like something palatable. But it was a crude drawing of a woman slumped against a tree with a knife sticking out of her chest. When she touched the information icon, it showed that it had been sent from a five-digit number—untraceable. Crap.

Thank God, Thirteen was far away. She didn't have time for this. She forwarded it to Oscar and to the kid's parole officer. Surely it violated some condition of his parole for car theft, didn't it?

She crammed the phone into her pocket, stooped to walk under the long, trailing branches, and slipped her shoes off. On the other side of the stream, a little meadow lay green and cool under the hot sun. She waded across, stopping in the middle to enjoy the clear, sparkling water as it murmured around her feet and over the rocks. On the other side, she sat cross-legged on the grass. Time to decide what to do.

Option one: Accept that Jean-Luc's collapse was a natural event and do nothing. The problem was, sudden respiratory arrest was unusual, and to her mind, suspicious. Option two: Tell the officer about her symptoms and concerns and urge him to investigate. Option three: Get a copy of the videos. See what Viane was doing when Jean-Luc collapsed. Check out the expression on her face, then go from there. Why hadn't she thought of that sooner?

She hurried back across the stream, laced on her shoes, and climbed up the hill to the B&B as fast as she could. Arielle should be able to get copies of the videos. At least one camera would have been focused on Viane when he fell. Her expression would tell a lot. Officer Chevalier would understand. These days, weren't all policemen trained in nonverbal communication?

But Arielle had not returned from the bank.

In the meantime, it was a few minutes before seven a.m. in Seattle, and Oscar generally arrived at the office by then. Britt sat in front of her laptop and opened a video call. "Be there, please." Oscar knew as much about criminal behavior as anyone on the planet. And she missed his friendship, their camaraderie. Somewhere deep inside, she had been hoping for an excuse to call him.

Oscar's wild, flyaway gray hair filled the screen, making his eyes, nose, and mouth look comically small in his long, rectangular face, like a little island in the middle of a wind-blown lake. He wagged his eyebrows, one up and one down, in his typical greeting. "Brittie!" he crowed. He knew she hated to be called that. "You look ravishing, my dear, dear friend. What color is that on your hair? Rhubarb? Radish? Anything but blonde?"

She laughed. She hadn't realized how much she missed his teasing and his corny humor.

He said, "No more blonde jokes, eh?"

"That's what I like about talking to you, Oscar. I don't even have to open my mouth. You fill in both sides of the conversation." She laughed again, simply because it felt good to laugh.

He squinted at her. "What did you do to your eyebrows? I hope it didn't hurt. What, did somebody do that thing with the threads, where they wind them around and pull them out?"

Britt wrinkled her nose. "How do you know about that?"

Oscar patted his thick, bushy brows. "I am *au courant* with fashion, although many would not believe that." He gazed at her for a moment. "You are worried about something."

"I am." The tension in her chest eased. She could always count on Oscar. She started to forgive him for giving the job she'd hung her hopes on to Martin Sherwood.

"What, too many swains in Provence swooning over your ravishing new look?"

"Not that I've noticed." She stopped smiling. "I just forwarded a drawing that popped up on my phone a little while ago. I also sent it to Thirteen's parole officer, but I'd like your advice—whether there's anything else I can do."

"I was hoping you were going to tell me the lovely

Arielle has accepted my standing proposal of marriage."

"Not so far. Actually, I have another problem. In the middle of the market this morning, a man named Jean-Luc Thibaudet collapsed. I think it's possible that he was poisoned, most likely by his wife."

"So, what's the problem?"

"She's the most popular person in town, the town's darling, in fact. So far, everybody thinks he had a heart attack. So, she's going to get away with it."

"You're a scientist, remember, not a cop."

"I talked to the local policeman. They grew up together, and he's deaf to any criticism of her. I doubt that he would even consider that she might sneeze without using her little linen hanky."

"You need to be okay with the fact that you may not agree with what the police choose to do or not do."

"I can't just let it go."

"Is this another case of your instincts?"

"Not totally. I performed CPR, and afterward I had some strange symptoms."

"Brittie, listen to me. You have to let the police handle it."

"A good man may die very soon, if he isn't already dead, and no one suspects a thing."

"Life is not always fair. Lots of people get away with murder. You need to learn that you are not able to fix everything."

"I can't just stand by and watch it happen."

"Here's what I worry about. You care too much. When you believe in something, you risk your heart and soul, and that's a good way to get hurt."

"I hear you, and I'll go back to the police, but first,

I need to figure out how she might have done it. Now, who is the best person to talk to about poisons?"

"I'll check around."

He gazed at her, frowning and tapping his fingers on the desk. After a silence that was remarkably long for Oscar, he and said, "Brittany Ann Thornton, look at me. Poisoners are the smartest. Do not put yourself in jeopardy. In a tiny village, word gets around. If what you suspect is true, this woman is dangerous."

Chapter Seventeen

Chevalier

The moment Oscar signed off, Arielle knocked, then stepped into Britt's room. She had a giant grin on her face. "I can't believe how fast this is going. I've arranged a cash transfer, and one minute after midnight the cheese shop will be mine."

Britt grinned back. "Brava! The apartment, too?"

"Yup. I came to get you. Monique is waiting to show us."

Britt closed her laptop. "Can you get copies of the videos you guys made this morning?"

"I'll get a copy after they're edited."

"NG. No good. I need them unedited, all three of them."

Arielle's eyebrows disappeared under her bangs. "Why?"

"When they edit them, they'll discard Jean-Luc's collapse."

Arielle stopped, her hand on the doorknob. "So?" A note of impatience crept into her voice. "Come on. Put your shoes on."

"I want to see the expression on Viane's face right at the moment when she knew Jean-Luc was in trouble."

"Why?"

"There's a good chance she poisoned him."

Arielle's voice filled with frustration. "What are you talking about?"

"Poison. It's the only thing that would explain why I felt so weird after I did CPR."

"I'm sure there's a logical explanation. The doctor will diagnose what happened."

"Poison is what happened. Oscar agrees."

Arielle frowned. "You've been talking to him?"

Britt tossed her running shoes under the bed. "Yup."

Arielle's eyes pleaded with Britt to drop this idiotic idea. "Seriously, Viane can be pretty intense, but she is not a murderess."

"Will you get the videos anyway, please?"

"I can't. The film crew left already."

"Rats! There must be a way to get them."

"Brittany Ann Thornton, are you crazy?"

Britt slid her feet into her sandals. This was a big day for Arielle, and she was spoiling it. "By the way, Oscar still wants to marry you."

Arielle stomped her foot. "Whoop-dee-freakin' doo. Another example of impaired judgment." She glared at Britt. "See—that's what happens when you spend too much time with psychopaths."

****

Viane paced. She had spent the entire afternoon in this uninspired waiting room, as a loving wife should. She had become intimately acquainted with every stain on the carpet, every scratch on the wooden chair legs, and every dog-eared magazine. She wanted to scream. Things had started off so well. Jean-Luc hadn't even noticed the anti-nausea medication she's slipped him at breakfast. She had topped the salad with his favorite peppers, and he'd eaten two immediately. Then everything went wrong. That interfering American woman. The medics. They had never mobilized so quickly before. And who could have expected Jacqueline's teacher to carry an epinephrine pen with her? Viane could not sit still.

She jumped when the nurse touched her elbow. "Madame, Doctor says you may see your husband for a minute or two."

Viane followed his pale-blue scrubs down the corridor to Jean-Luc's bed. It was not in a room, but in a niche, right under three pairs of watchful eyes in the nursing station. "His heart is beating on its own," the nurse said, "but the respirator must breathe for him."

Surrounded by machines and wires and monitors, Jean-Luc looked pale and diminished. She felt a tiny pang of regret. He was normally so robust. But except for the mechanical rise and fall of his chest, he did not move. Clearly, if they weren't keeping him alive, he'd be dead. Viane tiptoed to the head of the bed, bent, and kissed his forehead. It felt cool and dry.

When she turned around, a tall, red-haired man with bright green eyes stood there. A stethoscope hung around his neck. "Dr. Brusseau." He held out his hand. "I have reviewed Monsieur Thibaudet's lab results, and I find nothing to explain his condition. Does he have any serious allergies?"

"No." Viane shook her head. "Not that I know of. But anaphylactic shock can happen suddenly, I believe."

He gazed at her. "Can you think of any other potential cause for his illness?"

"Where is Dr. De la Fontaine?"

"He is on vacation."

"He would know if there was something. He has known my husband all his life."

"Do not worry, Madame Thibaudet. I have ordered more tests. I shall do my best to discover what made him ill."

Viane's heart raced. Her hands felt clammy and cold. She reminded herself to smile. Closing her eyes, she took a deep breath. "That is good news."

****

Britt was dying to find a way to get the videos, but she went along with Arielle. They examined the cheese cases, admired the stock of wines, and complimented Monique on the décor in the cozy apartment.

Then Britt slipped away, hoping to find Monsieur Chevalier, but he was not in his office. She walked around the square, eavesdropping on conversations in the shops and hearing again and again that Jean-Luc must have had a heart attack. She began to doubt her own perception of what had happened.

At last, she returned to the cheese shop to hang out with Arielle and observe Monique's methods of cutting and wrapping cheese, ringing up sales, and helping customers select wine for their evening meals. By the time Monique hung the closed sign on the door, Britt still debated silently about whether Viane had poisoned her husband, but the other two women were happy and excited, and they were all hungry.

She let Arielle's chatter flow over her as the trio crossed the square and up the stairs into Viane's restaurant. In the tiny lobby, she noted the warm yellow ochre walls above polished wooden wainscoting. A bouquet of cream-colored lilies stood on the counter by the cash register. She liked the understated elegance. She had to give Viane credit. The woman had class.

A server dressed in traditional black pants and long white apron led them to a table on the terrace, where silverware and glasses sparkled against the crisply starched cloth. Viane came out of the kitchen wearing a chef's jacket and tall white hat. "I shall send the best champagne I have, and I shall cook for you, the best I have in the kitchen. It is my thanks for helping my husband."

"Is Jean-Luc well, then?" Monique asked.

"He is not yet well, but he is resting at the hospital."

Monique crossed herself. "I pray for his return to health."

Britt said, "It's unfortunate that your video was interrupted. Will you edit it yourself?"

"Marcel will work on that with the film crew in Paris." Viane marched back to the kitchen.

Britt sat back in her chair. She needed to think. And in the meantime, she would follow Monique's example and pray for Jean-Luc's recovery. If only she thought it would help.

The waiter brought champagne flutes and an ice bucket, then a bottle of champagne, which he opened with a flourish. They toasted Arielle's acquisition and Monique's move to Roussillon, where she would open a new shop. As the bubbles burst on Britt's tongue, she felt the tension of the day start to ebb.

It had been hours, but seemed like days, since she watched Jean-Luc set up his market stall, even longer since he sat beside her and re-shaped the nose she had sketched. She took a deep breath. For now, he was in the safest place possible. She hoped Arielle was right. Maybe it wasn't poison. But first thing in the morning, she would have a serious conversation with Officer Chevalier.

Beginning with foie gras, then scallops in mornay sauce, course followed course out of Viane's kitchen, each superbly prepared, delicious, and accompanied by a different wine. At some point, Britt lost count. A sliver of a moon shone over Arielle's shoulder, and every minute more stars appeared in the warm Provençal sky. It was a lovely evening, and she was truly happy for Arielle and for Monique. One should always count her blessings.

One by one, the tables around them emptied until only they and a pair of men at the adjacent table were left, one with his back turned toward Britt. He stood and turned around.

Britt gasped. "Stan Gibson!"

"Hello, Britt. I need a word with you."

Immediately sober, she said, "I have no secrets, and even if I did, you've been eavesdropping all evening, so you might as well talk to me in front of my friends."

His brown eyes twinkled with amusement. "Fine."

He placed a photo in front of her—a picture of a shiny metal cylinder. They all leaned over it and stared. Judging by the size of the hand in the picture, it was as long as a man's forefinger. It had slits in two sides and flanges that looked like big round ears on top. "Do you know what this is?"

"Where did you get that?"

"The FBI office in Seattle sent it."

"Why?"

"Your husband—"

Britt offered him a scowl. "My ex, thank you very much."

"Your not-quite-yet ex claims he doesn't know what it is."

"Of course he knows what it is."

"Well?"

"It's a key. It opens a valve on a steam engine."

"Can you be more specific?"

"My father's favorite movie was the *African Queen*, so he built a one-half-scale replica of Humphrey Bogart's character's boat and named it *African Queen Two*. She runs on steam, just like the one in the movie, only it burns propane instead of wood. That key opens and closes the boiler valve, and that makes the boat go faster or slower."

"Where is she moored?"

"At the Seattle Yacht Club."

Stan gave a little bow. "Ladies, it's been a pleasure."

Chapter Eighteen

Chevalier

Britt listened to the deep, dense silence in the old stone B&B belonging to Monique's grandparents. The glowing green numbers on the clock beside her pillow mocked her attempts to fall asleep. 3:57 a.m.

Stupid. Stupid. Stupid.

Britt pulled the sheet up under her chin and squeezed her eyes shut. Why had she opened Rob's e-mail last night and read it? She should have trashed it the instant she saw it. Didn't she know he'd push all her buttons? Now his words looped through her brain like news scrolling across the bottom of the screen on television. "I have committed an appalling error. I hope you can find it in your heart to forgive me."

That was so Rob. Britt gritted her teeth. Making it sound as if he had made a teeny tiny mistake.

More of his drivel popped into her mind, "My love, think again about what you have done. You have set in motion a plan that will rip apart our beautiful family, the family of which you are the soul."

What a crock! Britt pulled her pillow over her head.

His words persisted. "Our daughter will have lost the beacon that she trusts to guide her."

In other words, for Megan's sake, I should stick

with him. Together we would smile at the world and say we have pulled together and overcome. I bet his attorney told him to write this. Of course. He'd look better in court if his loyal wife were there. How come I didn't see through him long ago?

"I will be lost in a stormy sea without a compass to point the way or a rudder with which to steer."

No shit. He won't need a compass where he's going. Or a rudder. Or the key to the *African Queen Two*. What was that about? Why did the FBI have it, and why on God's green earth did Stan Gibson think it necessary to drive all the way down from Paris to ask her what it was?

Britt sat up straight in bed, pulled her pillow onto her lap and pummeled it with both fists until, exhausted, she lay back down. She needed to sleep. In the morning, Arielle would go off to meet her wine tour group in Bordeaux, leaving her behind so she could learn how to operate the old-fashioned cash register in the cheese shop and start serving customers—with all of two years of high school French. More importantly, she must go to the hospital, talk to Jean-Luc, and find a way to tell him what she suspected—if he still lived.

Her brain refused to rest. Pink morning twilight filtered through the lace curtain on the window. Britt got out of bed. Bare feet brushing wide planks softened with age, she stepped across the tiny room, pushed the curtain aside, and leaned her forehead against the cool glass. Only one light showed in the entire circle of handsome old buildings that flanked the square. The town slept under fading morning stars, innocent of rage, or greed, or avarice.

Her host, Monique's grandfather, stood in the

square beside his motorcycle, fastening his helmet. He threw his leg over the bike and leaned forward to start it. The day had begun. With a sigh, Britt turned around and pulled her running shoes out from under the bed. She might as well go for a run. One thing she would *not* do today was open gruesome text messages on her phone.

****

Édouard Chevalier awakened with a start. Sometime during the night, it had come to him that Oscar Plitman's book, *Who Lies and Why*, stood on the shelf in his office, and the co-author's name was Brittany something. He remembered that because, at first, he'd confused the name with the region of Brittany in northeast France. Could it be Brittany Thornton?

Stars glimmered in the early morning twilight. He lay still for a while, watching them through his bedroom window at the top of the old farmhouse. An unsettling sense of foreboding swirled around his head. Would Viane harm her husband, Brittany asked. What kind of policeman would he be if he simply dismissed the question? But how preposterous! *Incroyable*! Even if Brittany was the same psychologist who worked with Plitman.

Viane might be unhappy, but she would not harm Jean-Luc. No. She would not. That might be the way in America, but here, in Provence? No. It was only the darkness that made him think the American woman could possibly be right.

The stars winked out of the gray-blue sky. The rooster crowed. Troubadour gave a soft meow and jumped to the floor. Édouard got out of bed, laced on his running shoes, and dismissed the cloud of doubt hovering over his head.

He would run across the valley to the wine co-op, circle back to town, and then, to challenge his aerobic capacity, sprint up the hill to the square. He settled into a steady pace. At this time of day, the air smelled cool and fresh. Pockets of ground fog lurked about in the low spots, occasionally thick enough to block the rising sun, in other places, thin and ethereal. The scent of cherries, red and heavy on drooping green boughs, told him they were ripe, ready to pick. The poppies along the road, now past their prime, had begun to yield to the lavender. At the wine co-op, he circled the low, square building, drew in an appreciative whiff from the bakery next to it, and headed on up the valley.

The hill on which Chevalier perched loomed before him. Fog hung heavy over the creek and, chased by the breeze, it rose up, obscuring the village. Monique's *grand-père* appeared in the oncoming lane, mist swirling about his motorcycle. Every morning he rode to the bakery for croissants and baguettes, which the baker was dragging out of brick ovens on long-handled boards right now. The older man lifted his hand in greeting, as did Édouard, and the sound of the bike faded away behind him.

****

At sunrise, Viane telephoned the hospital and learned that Jean-Luc had begun to breathe without the help of the respirator and that they were moving him to a private room. That stupid nurse expected to hear peals of delight and gratitude, and Viane did her best to accommodate him. Now, she gripped the steering wheel as tightly as she had gripped the phone.

Her stomach churned. She had barely slept. The newly minted Doctor Brusseau's bright green eyes frightened her.

Who could have known old Doctor de la Fontaine would be away? It would have been easy to convince the complacent old fool that Jean-Luc had been having symptoms of heart disease. She would have been home free. As it was, the normal toxicology screen at the hospital would not reveal what Jean-Luc had ingested, of that she was certain. But Brusseau said he would order more tests. What tests? What did he suspect?

Everything had conspired against her—the medics, that friend of Arielle's, even Édouard.

Thank the stars she had remembered to go back to the restaurant and retrieve her vials. She reached across the seat to reassure herself. Yes, they were in her purse. Safely stowed. Time to get to the hospital.

****

Britt followed the cobbled street down the hill to the bottom. Approaching the stream, she spotted another runner on the far side of the bridge, coming uphill. A car whooshed up behind her. Headlights dazzled in the fog and blinded her. She hugged the rail on the side of the bridge. As the big green sedan zoomed by, she saw slender white hands on the wheel. Viane. Driving much too fast, looking neither left nor right.

Britt continued on, but no one was there. Where was the other runner? They should have passed each other by now. What if Viane's car had struck him? He would have tumbled down the rocky, steep-sided ramp that raised the road to the level of the bridge.

Her heart thumped against her ribs as she called

out, "Helloo-oo-oo?" She stood on the side of the road and peered down.

"*Allo*," a strong, healthy voice replied. A head of very white hair materialized out of the fog, followed by shoulders and torso.

"Oh! Monsieur Chevalier."

He climbed up the rocks that formed the ramp. "*Oui. C'est moi.* Please, may you give me your hand?"

"Of course."

"I trust you are strong." He put one hand on the road and the other in hers. She pulled hard, leaning back to counterbalance his weight. He got a knee up on the road, then the other, and slowly, still gripping her hand, stood up. He took a step and winced. "*Mon dieu.*" He shifted all his weight to the other foot.

"Viane nearly ran over you."

"The mist came. It makes it impossible to see, so I jumped down onto the rocks."

"Ah, the mist." Was everyone in Chevalier blind?

He took a step but limped badly.

"Monsieur Chevalier, you are hurt."

"I wonder if I might try to walk with your help."

Britt slid her arm around his high, narrow waist, and pulled him against her, exactly as she would once have done for Rob.

"Ah, *merci*, Madame. I fear I must lean on you."

"Perhaps I should go get a car."

"I believe I can walk. Let us see." He limped, but without complaint. "You are a friend to help me. You must call me Édouard."

Monique's grandfather, returning from the bakery, roared up beside them and stopped. "My friend, you are hurt?" He shut down the motorcycle, got off, and removed the basket lashed to the seat behind him. "Madame, if you would be so kind," he said, handing the basket to Britt. A bouquet of baguettes poked their noses out from under the red and white checkered cloth. The smell of still-warm bread made her mouth water.

Édouard hopped to the bike and swung his injured leg over the seat where the basket had been. The motorcycle rumbled to life, and Britt watched his long narrow back disappear up the road into town. Hugging the basket, she resisted the urge to bite one of the pointy, crusty ends as she started back up the street. When she had nearly reached the B&B, Monique's grandfather came to meet her and took the basket from her. He led her to the garden behind the inn.

The policeman sat at a table covered with a red and white checkered cloth, his foot packed in ice and elevated on a chair. He laid a phone on the table. "I have good news. Jean-Luc has begun to recover."

They sat together, gazing out over the red tile roof of the building on the hillside below the B&B. The early rays of the sun felt as warm and soft as silk. Tiny bees buzzed around the lavender that bordered the yard and filled the air with fragrance. In the distance, Mount Ventoux sloped upward to meet the sun. Perhaps there was a God. Perhaps her prayers had been answered.

"It is beautiful, *n'est-ce-pas*?" Édouard spoke quietly, reverently.

"*Oui*, very beautiful." Britt sighed. "It is hard to believe that anything evil or even unpleasant could happen in such a lovely place, but I must tell you that after performing CPR yesterday, my lips were numb, and I felt weak and dizzy for some time. I very much fear that Jean-Luc was poisoned, and that I picked up some of the poison when I blew into his lungs."

His back jerked up straight. He shook his head. "I cannot think that poison made Jean-Luc ill or caused your symptoms."

"I'm not accusing Viane of poisoning him on purpose."

"Viane is very careful about the food that is prepared in her restaurant. Surely there are other explanations for the way you felt. The stress, the heat of the day, being in a foreign place; all of these things might have affected you."

"That is true, but you must consider the possibility of poison."

He frowned. "Madame, we must allow the doctor to decide what made Jean-Luc ill."

"Of course." He wasn't going to listen to a stranger. She needed to establish a connection with him. "Have you always lived here?"

Édouard nodded. "Yes, except for two years when my parents sent me to school in London, so I would learn properly to speak English."

"What was that like for you?"

He grimaced. "I have never wanted to go again. London is as cold and gloomy as Seattle." He was gazing at her, watching her face.

"Seattle?" she asked.

"I think you live there, yes?"

Maybe he wasn't just a small-town cop. "Yes."

"Then I remember correctly. I believe you wrote a book with Oscar Plitman, which is now used by officers everywhere, to know if someone is lying."

Britt sighed. Yes, she had written the book. No, she had not realized her husband was lying and bonking

Graciella right under her nose.

Monique's grandfather brought a large wicker tray with golden croissants, a thin, crusty baguette split lengthwise, marmalade, butter, orange juice that looked as if it had just been squeezed, and best of all, strong hot coffee and hot milk. He set it in front of them and hustled back toward the kitchen.

Édouard poured steaming milk and coffee together into a wide white cup and offered it to her with the lift of one pale eyebrow. "I notice that there has been a ring on your finger for a long time but you do not wear it now. I wonder why."

It was a fair question. He should ask. He should try to find out who she was, to learn what her motivation might be. But she so did not want to talk about the demise of her marriage. She sipped the coffee. "This is excellent. Have you tried it?"

"I am a policeman. I notice such details." His tone was conciliatory, but firm.

Clearly, if she wanted a bridge between them, it would have to go both ways. "I discovered recently that my husband is not the man I thought he was." As unexpected as rain out of a clear blue sky, words began to pour from her mouth, and she couldn't stop them.

He listened without interrupting, his pale blue eyes meeting hers from time to time, his expression grave and quiet.

At last, she paused and sat back in her chair. She felt as if a boulder had lifted off her chest. "I can't believe I have been jabbering at you, telling you my woes. I hardly know you." Tears threatened to puddle in the corners of her eyes. It had been hard to keep everything in, to hide her anxiety and moments of despair from Arielle.

Édouard smiled. "But, Madame Thornton, Brittany; may I call you that? It is not difficult to know me. I have lived all my life near the town founded by my great-great grandfather, in the farmhouse that my grandparents built when my father was yet an infant, and I play the oboe in our chamber orchestra. I play boules with the men in the village one night each week. You see? I am not a complicated man."

She did see. Bless him. A kind, thoughtful, intelligent man, with a big blind spot where Viane was concerned.

Chapter Nineteen

Chevalier

Monique's grandfather helped Édouard into the back seat of Monique's hatchback and propped his purple, swollen foot up onto an array of pillows. Britt started the engine. Monique would open the cheese shop. Britt would get back as soon as she could.

But only after she found Jean-Luc. Would he be glad to see her? Heat crept up her cheeks. What's up with this interest in other men? Other men. Rob would soon be her ex. Other men would simply be men. Men with whom she might exchange e-mail addresses and phone numbers. Jean-Luc. Édouard. Perhaps she would refer to them as "friends," perhaps as "an interesting man I met on vacation."

As they rumbled down the hill, Britt glanced in the mirror at her passenger. "When Jean-Luc's parents died, did anything change for Viane?"

He paused a moment before answering. "At the farm, the house and all the buildings were old and rundown." A tentative note crept into his voice. "She made it all look beautiful, like a farm in a storybook."

"Before that, did they live together with his parents?"

"*Oui.*"

"Ah." Britt felt a flood of empathy for Viane. That

could make a person a little crazy. No way would she want to live with her mother-in-law, even though she liked her.

"What would be different if Jean-Luc died?"

"Brittany, my friend." Édouard sounded impatient. "I shall talk to the doctor. I shall ask what made Jean-Luc ill. But I must tell you again. I do not believe Viane would harm anyone."

Britt pressed her lips together.

"You must let go of your suspicions."

He could be right, or not. The vision of Viane's stony face, her hands gripping the steering wheel as she sped across the bridge sent shivers down Britt's spine.

At the hospital, she helped him into the emergency room and then, with directions from a passing nurse, set off to find Jean-Luc.

She spotted him in a small white room with a large window facing a nursing station. Surrounded by monitors, tethered by wires and tubes, and propped up in bed, he faced a large arrangement of orchids and birds of paradise, which stood on a table at the foot of his bed. Britt halted in the doorway as Viane, her voice loud and shrill, poured out a torrent of French from behind the flower arrangement.

"*Non, non, non.*" Jean-Luc's tone was patient but firm. "*Je ne veux pas.*"

Britt backed away from the door. Viane stormed out of the room, her high heels pounding the polished stone floor, her cheeks flushed, her eyes bright and angry.

There was something he didn't want to do, and she was furious. She clasped a manila folder to her chest.

"*Bonjour,*" Britt said.

Viane stopped and put a hand to her forehead. "Brittany, I am sorry. This is terrible. My husband refuses to make his life easier. I am so distressed." She gripped Britt's hand. "You must forgive me. Please, come to my restaurant for your lunch." She hurried off.

Britt walked up and down the hall twice. Could she be totally wrong? Finally, she stopped at the door to his room, held her breath, and looked in.

His face lit up in a wide smile. His warm brown eyes welcomed her. "I am told you have saved my life." He held out his hand and gripped hers tightly. "I feel that I may call you Brittany. *Merci, merci beaucoup*, Brittany." He pronounced it Breetanee, rolling the r and accenting the last syllable. "It is kind of you to come."

"Not at all," she said. She gazed at his fingers, so strong and brown. Her whole hand had disappeared inside his. The tight, anxious knot in her chest started to unravel. A great sigh escaped before she could stifle it.

"When I fell to the ground, I thought I would die, but I looked up and saw the face of an angel. An angel. Breetanee."

The way he said her name sent a loopy, happy feeling to her heart. "How are you feeling?" Her hand did not hurry to leave his.

"I am well. It feels strange to me that I am here." He gazed at Britt for a moment. "My wife believes I collapsed because I work too hard."

"Do you agree?"

"*Non, non.* I work, but it is not hard. I make cheese in the manner of my father."

"Your father taught you how to make your cheeses?"

"*Oui.* Also fine hams. And it is good to carry on in

117

his tradition. Each Tuesday, I take them to the market in L'Isle-sur-la-Sorgue, the next day to Chevalier, and to Gordes each Friday. I see *tout-le-monde,* everyone. I meet old friends." He squeezed her hand. "I make new friends. It is a good life."

He smiled, and Britt felt herself falling into the depths of his dark chocolate eyes.

"If I would not do these things, then I would be *désolé*—do you understand?"

"*Oui*, you would be sorry, sad."

Jean-Luc nodded. "*Bien sur*. Yes, truly." He sighed. "I have patented my temperature control system which I use in the rooms where I age my cheeses and hams. If I would sell it as Viane wishes, there would be more money to keep at the bank in Chevalier. She says, perhaps then I will go on a cruise, you understand, or I could buy more cows and make more cheeses. But I do not wish for more money. I prefer to share freely what I know with others."

Britt bit her lip. How the heck was she going to tell him? "Were you surprised that you fell ill yesterday?"

"*Certainement*. I am never ill, even for a day."

"Your daughter was there. She tried to help you. She must have been frightened."

"*Oui*. She feared that I would die, as her mother did. But because you were there, I did not." He smiled again. "And you, Brittany, do you have children?"

"I have a daughter also. She is twelve now, almost a teenager." *And she texts me frequently to let me know I'm ruining her life.*

"A time when children can be difficult," he said.

"Yes. But I am fortunate. She loves to spend the summer with her grandmother, who lives in California.

It is good for both of them."

"I agree. I, also, am most fortunate. Jaqueline's grandparents care much for my daughter, and she for them."

"Viane's parents?"

"*Non.*" He looked pensive. "The parents of my wife. My first wife. Jacqueline's mother. They live but one farm away."

A tall, red-haired man with the bright green eyes knocked at the open door and walked in. He wore khaki slacks and a blue buttoned-down shirt with a navy tie knotted loosely at the throat. He looked barely old enough to shave. A stethoscope hung loosely from his hand, and he tossed it around his neck. "Ah, Monsieur Thibaudet."

Jean-Luc reached for Britt's hand and held onto it. "Doctor Brusseau, my friend is Brittany Thornton. It is she who saved my life. If you speak English, she may hear what you wish to say."

"Very well. I have reviewed your family history. It appears that both of your parents died of heart attacks."

"*Oui*, that is so."

"Had either of them been ill?"

"*Non.*"

"I have more questions. Have you traveled recently in the tropics?"

"*Non*, I have stayed in Provence."

"Have you eaten raw fish? Sushi, perhaps?"

"*Non, non*, I do not care for it."

"In the market yesterday, did you eat anything different or strange?"

"*Non, non.*" Jean-Luc paused, frowning. "But as I ate the small red peppers, which I love, I tasted ten cigars all at once."

Britt's hand went to her lips. "Tobacco. It was very strong." It was one of the poisons mentioned by Oscar's expert.

Doctor Brusseau turned to her. "You performed CPR?"

"Yes, and afterward, my lips were numb, and I felt weak and dizzy."

"Do you smoke or vape?"

"No."

"And you, Monsieur Thibaudet?"

"I smoke one cigar each day, and sometimes in the evening, I begin another."

"Madame, how long did your symptoms last?"

"My lips were numb, and I felt extremely weak for about twenty minutes, but after two hours, I felt fine again."

Doctor Brusseau gazed at Britt, then at Jean-Luc. "I shall order more tests."

Nicotine. Of course.

Chapter Twenty

Chevalier

X-rays showed three broken bones in Édouard's ankle. An orthopedic surgeon came in early to pin them together, so by late afternoon his cast was dry, and the anesthetic had dissipated enough to allow him to walk with crutches. However, his brain felt as jumbled and disorganized as a cluttered old attic, and he was grateful when Brittany returned to take him home.

But on the way home she peppered him with questions about Jean-Luc's family history. "This morning, Dr. Brusseau asked Jean-Luc how his parents died, and he said both of them had heart attacks. And today, everyone in the village thinks Jean-Luc did also. I wonder if there is a pattern."

"I wondered also, and I asked Jean-Luc's doctor while I waited for you to pick me up."

"When his parents died, was anyone present who had been trained to perform CPR?"

"As I was not there myself, I cannot say."

"Then perhaps it is possible that they also stopped breathing before their hearts stopped." She paused, frowning, gazing in the mirror. "That would be a rather large coincidence."

He frowned. "*Oui. Oui,* if that were so, it would be a great coincidence." He did not appreciate her questions. "But it is not so. You cannot come to our little town and assume that we don't know when someone has a heart attack." He pulled in a breath, tried to tamp down his irritation. He would be patient. After all, she had helped him today, and she had rushed to help Jean-Luc while others stood and gaped. "They were older. A heart attack would be normal."

"So, they were older than most parents?"

"*Non, non.* But old." As patiently as he could, Édouard explained. "The three cases are not at all alike. His father's heart had a defect, which probably caused his heart attack. His mother was also diagnosed with a heart attack, but many believe she died of grief. Jean-Luc's heart shows no defect. And he did not die. So, you see, Brittany, there is no pattern."

In the mirror, her brow wrinkled in a frown. He frowned back. "His own doctor will be back tomorrow. He has known the Thibaudet family for many years, and he will diagnose Jean-Luc's illness. I assure you of this. Perhaps, in America, poisoning happens, but in Chevalier? *Non.* In all of Provence. *Non.* As I have told you before, you must not imagine such a thing."

With a mixture of relief and gratitude, Édouard watched Brittany drive off. True, all three of the Thibaudets had collapsed, but they were absolutely not the same. No one had been poisoned. He pushed the implications of her questions aside as he hopped into the kitchen. He had something very important to consider.

She had told him Monique would bring his dinner. He opened the pantry door and, leaning his crutches on a shelf, reached up high for the ancient silver sugar bowl. He turned it upside down, and his grandmother's ring fell into his hand.

He hopped to the kitchen window and held it up to the light. Nestled in a wide gold band and flanked by smaller stones, the large, square-cut yellow diamond sent shards of rainbow light dancing over the ceiling. In the morning, he would take it to town to get it cleaned and resized.

It didn't matter that he had always thought it was beautiful. It only mattered what Monique thought. Perhaps she would prefer a new setting, something modern. Whatever she would like, she should have.

At the moment, his foot throbbed, and he felt short of breath. Slipping the ring into his shirt pocket, he went outside and sat on the old wood bench under the cherry tree near the kitchen door. He turned a bucket upside down and propped his foot up on it.

When Monique arrived, she lifted a basket out of the back of her car and walked down the path beside the house. She sat beside him for a minute, asked about his foot, and then went inside. He could see her through the open door, moving from the sink to the stove as easily as she did in her own kitchen. She wore a short, soft, knit dress which wrapped snugly around her slender hips and hugged her breasts. How beautiful and graceful she was!

He could not ask her to marry him while she waited on him. What impression would that make? No, he must wait, no matter how urgently he desired her answer. Tomorrow, he would cook for her. And then he would propose.

She placed a lid on a large pot on the stove and came outside. "It only needs to get hot now." She sat beside him.

He took her hand and asked her to stay the night.

"I must go close up the shop, and I am tired."

He realized with surprise that it had been some time since she had stayed.

"I have received an offer to buy my store." Monique tilted her head and gazed at him the way she did when she wanted to know what he was thinking.

Always, she considered him. He would never find a more gracious, more fitting woman to be his wife. What a fool he had been! How fortunate a fellow he was, to have Monique with whom he got on so well, for so many years. "Do you mean someone wishes to buy it? How extraordinary!"

"*Oui*, it is unusual, perhaps, but Arielle McGregor wishes to live here and to have a small shop with cheeses and wine and other fine Provençal products. It is what she and her husband dreamed to do."

"*Eh bien*, a shop just the same as your shop?"

"Exactly."

"She should look in Apt, where I know there is one for sale."

Monique's smile looked wistful. "Her husband has died, and she wishes to fulfill the dream they had together." She said it very softly, with the same hint of wistfulness in her voice.

She got up and went into the kitchen. In a few minutes, she brought him a tray to balance on his knee, with a plate full of osso bucco over potatoes mashed in their skins, all in a rich dark sauce. The scents of garlic and parsley wafted up at him. "Ahhh," he said, "food for a prince."

She smiled again.

"You are tired, Monique."

"Yes."

She returned carrying a glass of wine for herself. "I will stay until you have eaten, and then I will go."

Édouard dug his fork into the rich braise and raised it to his mouth, then put it down. "But you must have some."

"No, I only want a glass of wine. I am not hungry."

"*Bien.*" Again, he raised his fork to his lips but paused. "You are well?"

"*Oui.* Of course. You must eat while it is hot."

She sat beside him, and the shadows cast by the olive trees grew longer. The light took on a golden glow of evening. A soft breeze fanned their faces.

Monique took the tray when he had finished and came back with espresso and chocolate. "I will go now," she said. She kissed him lightly on the top of his head and strode away beside the house, down the path to her car.

He sipped the espresso, his heart full of love and gratitude. Tomorrow he would buy a bottle of her favorite champagne, and he would roast a chicken. A roasted chicken with lemon and rosemary. New potatoes also. That was not difficult. She would sit down, and he would present the dinner to her, but first—yes, first, he would present the ring and ask her to give him her hand.

They would begin the future. Their future.

Chapter Twenty-One

Chevalier

Viane cinched her silk robe around her waist and glared out the kitchen window at the gleaming new campervan her mother, Térèse Stephanopolous, had driven up to the door. For the last three weeks, it had been parked out of sight from the farmhouse, at the far end of the cherry orchard, her preferred place when she stayed in Chevalier. She refused to say how she afforded a new campervan, but Viane suspected Jean-Luc had helped her.

It was too annoying to find her mother in the kitchen, drinking coffee, as if she owned the place. She should have locked the doors last night. "If you are going to start picking tomatoes in Spain tomorrow, don't you need to leave?"

"Soon." Térèse grinned, showing yellowed teeth in her wrinkled, nut-brown face. She parked her tall, skinny body on a stool beside the counter, clearly not in a hurry. "I'm curious."

Viane folded her arms on her chest. "So?"

Her mother had that expression on her face, like a cat taunting a mouse. "Your husband did not die."

Viane's fingers tightened on the coffee cup. "Correct."

Térèse showed her ugly teeth again.

Her mother had always had the ability to perturb her, but she would not give her the satisfaction of showing it. She merely waited.

"He will recover?" The knowing look in the small black eyes was meant to convey some kind of superiority.

"Yes, he will recover." She kept her expression bland, as if her mother had merely wondered aloud if it would rain today.

The old woman smirked. "How inconvenient!"

"What is inconvenient is to find you lurking in my kitchen." She turned away to hide her frustration and contempt. "Drink your coffee, *Maman*, and go. I must prepare for work."

****

Britt stood in the dim, cool alcove at the back of the cheese shop. All along the wall, from floor to ceiling, bottles of wine lay on their sides waiting to be opened, swirled and sniffed, then tasted. But this morning, she did not relish their lush, latent promise.

A text message had popped up on her phone as soon as she got up. Another crude cartoon. Like the first one, it had come from a throwaway device. It didn't matter. She knew the kid who called himself Thirteen had sent it. This time, it was a woman sitting at a desk with a knife sticking out of her chest. Her face was a caricature of Britt's and/or his mother's.

—*Hahaha. Hahaha. Hahaha.*—

At first thought, it was a threat, and it made her blood run cold. But perhaps it was something different. Maybe, in his twisted mind, he had decided she understood him, and he wanted to share an accomplishment. Perhaps it meant "See what I did?"

Not threatening—but boasting.

She reminded herself to breathe through the tightness in her chest as she looked at it again. The cartoon figure was seated, not at a table, as she had been when she interviewed him, but at a desk. Clearly, it was a desk, like a teacher's desk, with books and a little vase of flowers on one corner. This was not about her. What if he had killed again and was gloating?

She had forwarded a copy to Oscar, who answered promptly that there had been no murders in the area, at least none that weren't already accounted for, that Thirteen had met with his parole officer just yesterday, and that he continued to meet the requirements of his car-theft-related parole. In fact, the kid was getting on well at his job stocking shelves at the local big box store.

So, maybe there was another meaning. Regardless, the drawing gave her palpitations. To calm her racing heart, she reminded herself that he was far away on another continent. And that Oscar had promised to dig around and to learn what he could about the messages and about Thirteen. For now, she must leave the kid to her mentor. She must focus on Viane.

Her brow wrinkled in concentration, Britt slipped a freshly starched white apron over her head and reached behind her back to tie the strings. She wandered out of the alcove into the store. How many killers did she know of? Murderers who felt that killing was justifiable, or even a pleasurable act. Several? A few? Was Viane like any of them?

Several well-known cases came to mind. Some, especially some serial killers, did it for the sake of killing, probably for the pleasure it gave them. But this was different. The act of murder would not reward Viane.

She wanted a restaurant in Paris. Obsessively? Perhaps. And Jean-Luc refused to provide the cash she needed to buy it. Seriously, would anyone in their right mind think it justified killing her husband? In the bright light of morning, it seemed improbable, but all the same, an icy hand brushed Britt's spine.

She had spent long hours in the night worrying, wishing she had found a way to warn Jean-Luc. And at the same time, she could visualize Oscar, his pipe clamped between his teeth, his fly-away hair billowing about his head, reminding her that she could be mistaken.

She frowned in concentration. Pray God Oscar was right. But was he?

"*Bonjour*, Brittany." Monique's voice startled her, and she jumped. Then she realized that although she had unlocked the door and opened it, she was standing in the doorway, blocking it.

Monique, who carried a bundle of baguettes, was waiting to come in. Behind her stood the twin eighty-year-old sisters whom she had seen sitting on a bench in the square the day before. They wore sturdy shoes and freshly ironed flowered dresses. One looked cranky and the other amused.

Britt stepped back. "Omigosh, please, come in. *Entrez, entrez.*" She beckoned with her hand. "I was thinking." She tapped a finger to her forehead. "*Je pense.*" The older women greeted her, one with a smile and the other with a scowl. They waited, one patiently, the other not, for her to bring the large wedge of Gruyère from the case and cut two thick slices.

Monique began to prepare sandwiches of butter, cheese, and ham on chunks of crunchy baguette. Leaving the ends bare, she wrapped a length of parchment paper around the middle of each one, skewered it with a wooden pick, and placed it in a growing pyramid in the cold case. As she worked, she coached Britt, who cut and wrapped little white packets of cheese, weighed them, and calculated the price for a steady flow of customers. This demanded all of Britt's attention.

Normally, she would have loved to learn the names, the textures, the smells, the characteristics of all the cheeses. She would even have liked to discover how to ring up a sale on the old-fashioned cash register. But today she felt way too stressed. Her head ached, and her back felt stiff and sore. Really, why couldn't they have a scale that did all that automatically? Why couldn't they at least have a cash machine that calculated the change?

Arielle had laughed at the suggestion. "The customers trust that big old cash register. They like that it's crusted with gold trim and that a bell rings when you open the drawer. Having the store owned by an American is a huge change for them. Don't even think about new machines."

Well, Arielle should just come and try it for herself instead of traipsing around in a minibus, tasting wine with a bunch of happy vacationers.

Around eleven o'clock, the shop grew quiet, empty. Monique cleaned the marble countertop, gathering baguette crumbs in a damp white cloth. "Enough sandwiches," she said. She pronounced it "saand-weeches."

For the first time, Britt looked closely at her companion. Monique had dark purple half-moons under her eyes, and her face looked pale. "You seem tired, Monique," she said. "Are you all right?"

"*Oui*, I am well. I only stayed up late last night to finish packing for my move. I shall get coffee now." She smoothed back tendrils of hair that had escaped the auburn knot at the back of her head and walked briskly out of the shop.

Alone, Britt thought again of Thirteen. According to Oscar, he had an uncanny charm, which he turned on when it suited him, when he was in front of the judge, for instance. Probably, that was what got him off. Well, he had not charmed her. She shivered. Any woman with even a tiny grain of sense would shy away from him.

Similarly, Viane, with her wide-eyed, innocent look and dimpled smile, had charmed Chevalier. No one considered that she might try to poison Jean-Luc.

Monique returned carrying two white espresso cups, saucers balanced on top to keep them warm. She set them on the counter beside the cash machine, pulled out a pair of stools, and gestured that Britt should take one. As they sipped the strong, hot coffee, Viane's big forest green sedan rolled past the store, headed toward her restaurant on the far side of the square. Monique stared after the car. Her hands clenched into fists.

Britt's eyebrows went up. "It seems that Viane is a celebrity in this town. Everyone loves her."

Monique's face whipped around. "Viane! Viane! Viane! Ever since I came to this town, I have lived my life in her shadow. That is why I sold my shop. That is why I am leaving." Her cheeks turned bright red. "*Vielle vache*! Old cow! Everyone says how she is

131

wonderful, but I cannot say good things for her. Do you know that she killed her father?"

A chill prickled the back of Britt's neck and ran all the way down her spine.

Monique barely paused to take a breath. "No, I can see that you do not. But it is true."

"How did she kill him?"

"With a big pan from the kitchen. She hit him on the head, and he died."

"When?"

"When she was seventeen. Before I came to Chevalier."

"Why?"

"She said she did it to stop him from killing her mother. Everyone knew he beat her. So, everyone believed." Monique sucked in a huge breath. "But I believe she plans everything—everything. She will scheme until she gets what she wants. And she is greedy. She will never release from her grasp what she does not want."

"What she does not want?" Britt echoed.

Monique turned red, but she did not avert her gaze. "Everyone knows I am the woman scorned."

"Please tell me about that."

The man from the post office came in, removed his hat, and tucked it under his arm. He chatted with Monique in rapid French while she placed a sandwich on a plate. Still talking, he carried his lunch outside and sat at on one of the small round tables in front of the shop. He was followed by another man, then another, and Britt got absorbed in ringing up sandwiches.

Édouard came in, carefully lifting his cast over the threshold and swinging his crutches through. "I am happy to tell you that Jean-Luc will come home today. The doctor has determined that he suffered a heart attack, but it was not serious."

Britt stopped and stared. "A heart attack? Truly? But when I was there, Dr. Brusseau didn't think so. And you and I both know Jean-Luc stopped breathing before his heart stopped."

"*Oui*, my friend. I cannot explain it. But his own doctor, Dr. De La Fontaine, is at the hospital now. He has known Jean-Luc since he was a child."

"Dr. Brusseau said he would order tests for toxins. Did Fontaine say what those tests showed?"

Édouard shook his head. "He did not speak of them, so I must assume they confirmed his diagnosis."

Frowning, Britt put Édouard's sandwich in a small bag so he could carry it with his crutches. She wanted to talk privately with him, but Monique slipped into the wine room and stayed, as if searching for a bottle of wine that did not wish to be found, leaving her to serve the customers.

Édouard hovered near the cash register, glancing toward the back as if looking for Monique, while Britt rang up two more sandwiches. Then he left.

She stuck her head around the corner and whispered, "He's gone now."

Monique's face colored, and Britt wished she had pretended not to notice her disappearance. "I'm sorry," she said. "*Désolée*. It's not my business."

Finally, as the lunch crowd tapered off, Britt went back to the conversation about Viane. "Why did she marry Jean-Luc, do you think?"

"He bought the brasserie for her as a wedding gift."

"You think she married him for that?"

Monique gave a short, derisive snort. "*Oui.* Of course."

"Were you living here when Jean-Luc's parents died?"

"*Oui.*" Monique pressed her lips together for a moment. "Everyone said how sad it was that they were gone, and Viane went about, accepting condolences with big sad eyes. But I knew she was happy they were gone. It was in her face whenever she thought no one was looking."

Britt tipped her head to one side and thought a moment, then spoke very softly. "Do you think it possible that she poisoned them?"

Monique's eyes opened wide. The color drained from her face. "I hope not. But I must say, truly, she will always want more. That is how she is."

"You said you are a woman scorned."

"*Oui.* Édouard expected Viane to marry him. I did not know."

"Did you fall in love with him?"

Monique took a deep breath and stared out the open door at the square for several beats before turning back to look at Britt. She shrugged and smiled ruefully. "Édouard is a good, kind man. He is intelligent and interesting to talk to. I started playing my flute in the musical society we have in our town, where he plays the oboe. He was fun and funny and, after we played the music, he would say, would you care to have dinner together. And I did, many times, and then I hoped he would love me. And I told myself he did. And I loved him." While she talked, Monique poured two glasses of wine and set two sandwiches on plates.

She sighed again, a sound full of sadness. "But at

last, I knew he still loved her. And so, I am going away to live in Roussillon. Last night, when I brought him his dinner, I tried to tell him I am going. But I couldn't. Tonight, I must."

****

In the brasserie kitchen, Viane worked beside Gascon, the chef who ran the restaurant when she was in Paris. She hummed as she browned half a dozen lamb shanks and transferred them to an oval roasting pan while carrots, onions, and celery caramelized on another burner.

The fact that her mother lied in court all those years ago had always irked her. The judge would never have convicted her. Her story of her father's abuse had been a perfect defense. But no, her mother had to tell a convoluted tale and then take credit for the acquittal. Viane added the caramelized vegetables to the lamb shanks, tossed in a handful of herbs, and poured a bottle of red wine over it all.

But now, the knowing look in her mother's eyes was nothing to fear. The fact that she had committed perjury would keep her quiet. Viane put the lid on the roasting pan and tucked it into the oven. If she went down, *Maman* would go with her.

Why worry? Although Jean-Luc's survival had frustrated her at first, it was working out perfectly. Dr. De La Fontaine, that dolt, had decided Jean-Luc must have inherited an arterial defect from his father, and that had caused his collapse. Thank God! Now, if he had another attack, no one would question it. She hugged herself as she walked to the refrigerator and pulled out the pot of *coq au vin* she had started the day before.

Best of all, when she told the German sausage makers, Gustave and Gunther Mueller, that Jean-Luc was too ill to sign the papers, they had extended the agreement until he was well again. Perfect. She had a little window of time.

In three more days, she would cater the fundraiser for the church. Raising money for a new roof was Jean-Luc's idea, so he would certainly attend, and he would work hard to set up all the tables and chairs. Everyone would say it was inevitable that he would collapse again, that he shouldn't have exerted himself so soon. Perfect. Perfect. Perfect.

She would sign his name on those contracts—she could reproduce his signature perfectly—and date them the day before he died. Gustave and Gunther would hand her a boatload of money, and the *Cochon Qui Rit* on rue Saint-Dominique would be hers. She was on her way to three Michelin stars.

This thought buoyed her up all morning. Even the tedious task of stirring the risotto didn't annoy her.

When the lunchtime crowd at the brasserie petered out and most of the tables were empty, Viane took off her chef's jacket, walked across the square, and entered the cheese shop. "*Bonjour*, Monique, *mon amie*." She smiled across the store to the counter where Monique and Brittany sat on high stools eating sandwiches.

There was a tiny pause while both of them stared at her, eyes wide, and then they chorused, "*Bonjour*, Viane."

They had been talking about her. That's what that look meant. No matter. Let them talk. In a very short time, she would shake off the dust of this miserable town. She would live in the mansion in Paris, and the

Cochon Qui Rit would soar right to the top of the list of places to eat and drink and be seen.

She smiled again. "Monique, my dear friend, I want to thank you for storing my husband's hams and cheeses when he fell ill. I must go this evening to Paris to work on the videos we made in the market, but I will be back soon. When I return, I would like to cook for you. Will you come to lunch one day? In fact, both of you, please."

The stupid American had no idea how helpful she had been. Viane would reward her with a magnificent presentation of grilled lamb chops.

Chapter Twenty-Two

Chevalier

As the heat of afternoon waned, the stream of customers slowed to a trickle. It seemed to Britt that she had been on her feet forever, hustling from cheese case to cash register, struggling to understand and to make herself understood. Now, instead of cheese, most people were shopping for wine. Monique seemed to enjoy helping them choose, asking what they planned to serve for dinner and suggesting options.

Britt listened and watched and felt grateful that no one asked her opinion. Rob had always chosen the wines. What Britt knew about wine was that if she liked it, she drank it. And after an entire day of stuffing facts about seventy-three different cheeses into her brain, she had no more capacity. Learning about the wines would have to happen on another day.

Her attention wandered. Outside in the square, a pair of old men sat on a bench near the fountain, talking, gesturing, smoking, looking as if they had taken root there. Soon another joined them. Four wrinkled, gray-haired women in cotton dresses sat hip to hip on another bench, chatting, two of them knitting.

They looked as if they had been doing this for years. Perhaps they had lived here all their lives. Perhaps they had been friends all that time. Britt felt a little stab of envy, or maybe it was a sense of longing. How nice it would be to have lifelong friends to sit with every evening, to share the joys and trials of the day, and go home feeling that all would be well.

No wonder Arielle loved this little town. Édouard Chevalier loved it, too, and wanted to keep it the way it was. Something told her Jean-Luc did as well.

It must be different for Viane. Clearly, she preferred Paris. She couldn't picture Viane sitting on that bench in the square, not even when she was old. No, the traditions, the simplicity, the sameness of one day following the other would stifle her. Yet earlier, when Viane came over to thank Monique and invite them both to lunch, she practically purred with satisfaction.

She was up to something. Britt wished she could convince Édouard to at least consider the possibility of poison. *If I had a murder meter, it would be pegged on high. I am going to have to nail her butt. But how?*

When Monique finally pulled down the blind on the door of the shop, indicating it was closed for the day, she handed the key to Britt. "It's Arielle McGregor's now," she said. Clearly, it was a bitter-sweet moment. It marked the closing of a chapter in Monique's life, a chapter she had relished.

Britt watched her walk across the square and offered a silent blessing on her path forward. Then she locked the door and climbed the long, steep, stone steps leading to the apartment above, thinking that, even though Arielle wasn't there, this marked the beginning of a new chapter for her too.

Monique had left the apartment spotless. Except for the bathroom and a tiny bedroom furnished with twin beds, there was only one room. The kitchen consisted of a blue tiled counter with shelves above and appliances tucked underneath. Together with some bookshelves, it occupied one wall. On the opposite side, a small sofa and two wing-backed chairs upholstered in a muted sunflower pattern faced each other across a low table. In between, a kitchen table painted blue stood under the window that looked out onto the square. The whole thing would have fit in Britt's family room. Britt stood for a moment, looking around. Then she started to smile. The cheerful colors and the warm yellow limestone walls made it feel cozy. It was perfect for Arielle.

She lifted her suitcase onto one of the narrow beds and pulled out her laptop, then turned it on as she carried it to the table by the window. When her browser opened, she typed in "Viane Stephanopoulos trial." A list of links scrolled down the page, and a moment later, she was gazing at a photo of Viane, age seventeen, standing beside her mother. Except for the lines at the corners of her mother's mouth and eyes, they looked like sisters, with the same bony frame and thin face. In the fifteen years since then, Viane had blossomed into a round, full, voluptuousness. But she still held her head and shoulders as if balancing a crown.

The most interesting thing about the photo was the way they leaned together, not touching, but each mirroring the stance and posture of the other, clearly connected at the moment when the shutter caught them. But while her mother's eyes defied the cold, hard gaze of the camera, Viane's mocked it.

With some difficulty, Britt translated the text that followed. In court, Viane's lawyer argued that her father, an alcoholic and a mean drunk, had a habit of beating his wife. Her mother claimed that when Viane intervened one evening, he came at her with a knife. In self-defense, she hit him with a heavy pan. He stumbled backward down a flight of stairs and died of head injuries.

Britt toggled back to the photo. Viane's mother's face showed a wary kind of relief. Viane's leaked delight. Delight. Huh. Maybe, as Monique suggested, she planned to kill him. What if she provoked his attack? If she did, and got away with it, she would have found it easier to arrange for Jean-Luc's parents' deaths.

Britt pictured the mansion where Viane lived when she was in Paris and the carriage house where she recorded her podcasts. Would she have murdered Jean-Luc's parents for that? One thing was certain: People killed for less.

So, exactly how did his parents die? That was a place to start.

According to the officer, both of them had heart attacks. Nothing strange about that. Happens all the time. Britt typed, "Thibaudet, Chevalier, death, obituary." Five links came up, two about Gaspard Thibaudet; three about Martine Thibaudet, including a photo of her wearing a dour expression and an apron over a housedress.

Britt opened the translator app on her phone and struggled through the articles. Gaspard, Jean-Luc's father, died at his own birthday party. Question: Had Viane prepared the food?

A short time later, his mother died at a church dinner of some kind, catered by Viane. Britt went back over the articles, but there was no mention of respiratory arrest.

Unless they were trained in CPR, the birthday guests and church people wouldn't have known the difference between cardiac arrest and respiratory arrest. The medics wouldn't know which happened first, because by the time they arrived, their hearts would have stopped regardless. So, the diagnosis of heart attack made perfect sense.

At the end of the final article on Martine's death, a short paragraph stated that Jean-Luc had inherited his parents' farm at Chevalier, which he now owned in addition to his own small farm, and his grandmother's home in Paris. Huh! His grandmother left enough money to maintain the house ad infinitum, and to pay her housekeeper to take care of her ten cats as long as any of them were still alive. She must have been a little nutty, not to mention rich. Ten cats? Yes, *dix chats*, plain as a wart on the end of your nose.

Back in Paris, when Marcel picked Britt up and took her to watch the filming of Viane's podcast, there were several cats lounging on the balcony of the house. He said it had belonged to the grandmother, now departed, and crossed himself. Holy cow! It wasn't just a house. It was mansion in the center of Paris. It had to be worth millions.

What did she know so far? Britt cupped her hands over her eyes and rested them in the darkness of her palms. On the surface, it sounded far-fetched. She could be wrong—or worse yet, as Arielle claimed, barking mad. But she couldn't shake the idea.

All three family members had collapsed in front of a group of people. If Viane had prepared her father-in-law's party, then all three had been eating food she served. What if all three of them had suffered respiratory arrest before cardiac arrest? And what if the cause was poison? An accident? A coincidence? Not. No matter what Édouard Chevalier or anyone else said or believed.

The likelihood of *accidental* poisoning had to be somewhere around one in a billion. Well, maybe not quite, but way up there.

If Jean-Luc had left the hospital, then he was no longer surrounded by an attentive medical staff. Could that be why Viane looked so pleased this afternoon? If Britt was wrong, no problem. If she was right, his life was at grave risk.

Right or wrong, how on earth would she prove anything? She needed facts, and she had none. Perhaps if she could get a breath of fresh air, she could think. She headed for the stream and the tiny green meadow at the bottom of the hill. The big question: if Viane murdered the senior Thibaudets, how would anyone prove it at this late date?

As Britt ducked under the trailing branches of the willow, her phone quacked like a duck, which meant a phone call, so she pulled it out of her pocket. An unknown number. She stared at it. What if it was Thirteen, reaching out to her? Her mouth went dry, and her heart banged against her ribs. Only one way to find out. She touched the green button and tried to steady her voice. "Hello."

"Stan Gibson here." Stan, the FBI guy in Paris.

Frozen in place at the edge of the stream, and almost too surprised to speak, she squeaked out, "Hello, Stan."

"Brittany, I thought you would want to know that the agents in Seattle have found the missing money—the two-and-a-half million dollars."

"Finally." Her knees wobbled with relief. She had tried not to worry, but Stan's threat had been there, in the back of her mind, all this time, haunting her. "Where was it?"

"In Rob's tackle box, tucked away in the back of the *African Queen Two*."

"That's not a very original hiding place."

"Actually, it was. You know that place on Lake Union where they store boats up on elevated racks?"

"I've seen it."

"It seems he took the *Queen* out of his moorage at the Seattle Yacht Club and stored it under a fictitious name, way up on the top tier. It was not easy to find. Looking at it from the ground, it was very difficult to identify."

"I had no idea he was so creative."

"Indeed. Without significant pressure on his little friend, Graciella, we might never have found it."

Britt's stomach contracted. Graciella had that effect on her. "Shall I assume she is implicated in this?"

"She's in it up to her little neck. My guess is that they were planning to escape to a tropical island with the loot."

Britt sighed. How could she have been so blind, so stupid, so obtuse? How long had all of it been going on right under her nose?

"Perhaps you will enjoy your vacation more now that you are off the hook—well, unless someone decides that you participated in some other way."

"I had no part of it." She pushed the threat away.

"Actually, I'm glad you phoned me. I need your help."

"Help?"

"It's about Viane Thibaudet. You ate dinner at her restaurant when you came down to ask me about the boat key."

"It was good, too, delicious, in fact. So?"

"I think she poisoned her husband the first day I was here, in the market, right in front of a bunch of people."

"Let me guess—the reason it hasn't hit the news is that no one suspects a thing." His tone dripped skepticism.

"Exactly. How did you know?"

"A little birdie told me. I also know you performed CPR." There was a wry twist in his voice. "What makes you think I can or will help you?"

"You are a lawman."

"I have no jurisdiction in France."

"Stan, listen, I'm not asking you to arrest her. She was filming a video for her podcast, which she hopes to get on TV, so there were three cameras. At least one of them had to be focused on her at all times, and her expression will speak volumes."

"Theoretically."

"Not just theoretically. This is my area of expertise, and I want to see the discs before she has a chance to erase them."

"So?"

"The problem is, they are in Paris."

"And I am in Paris. Therefore, you think I should get them for you."

"As they say around here, *oui*. Right away. Please."

"*Non*, as we say around here." His voice was a dry as a popcorn fart.

He wasn't going to help. No one was going to help. Britt could barely breathe. "Please, Stan. Viane is coming up tonight to approve the way the film crew edited them, and if she does, they will surely delete the part where he collapsed. The evidence will be gone."

"I can't interfere. The job of the FBI in France is to help solve and prevent international crime. This is a matter for the French police. If you truly believe this, you have to convince the local law to step in."

"Stan, I'm begging you. The local police force consists of a very nice man who is completely blind to the possibility that his childhood sweetheart would commit murder. And I believe she will try again soon."

"The FBI cannot get involved."

"A good man is going to die, and you won't help me." Britt jabbed the red button on her phone and stuffed it into her pocket.

Chapter Twenty-Three

Chevalier

Édouard's crutches only hindered him, slowed him down. Fortunately for him, he was good at hopping. He had opened all the windows, and the evening breeze wafted through the old stone house, refreshing the hot, dusty, closed-up air. On the flagstone terrace just outside the kitchen door, the hen was already turning on the barbecue. Soon the scent of chicken stuffed with rosemary and orange would fill the air. Édouard hopped to the sink. He needed to wash the new potatoes and lay them in a pan under the roasting bird so that they would catch the juices and cook in them, slowly, exactly the way Monique liked them.

Everything would be perfect by the time she arrived. The ring, in a tiny silk pouch, lay in the bottom of his shirt pocket, which he had carefully buttoned. Just to make sure, he patted his pocket again with his free hand. Yes, safe.

By the time Monique parked in the shade beside the barn, even the ice bucket with the champagne and his grandmother's crystal flutes, glasses so delicate that he seldom dared take them from the shelf, were ready, standing on the tree stump beside the swing under the grape arbor.

As he poured champagne, Monique said softly, "I

have something I must tell you."

"But first, I have something I must ask you." He undid the button that closed his shirt pocket. "This is for you." He could barely breathe as he folded her fingers over the little silk package. Awkwardly, he got down on his good knee. He held her hands with both of his. "Please, tell me that you will marry me."

Monique's mouth opened, but no sound came out. She stared at him and then looked down at their hands. "Édouard, I don't know how to tell you." She gazed into his eyes.

"Say yes. Monique, say yes."

"I have loved you for a long time," she said.

Édouard released her hand. "And I love you. Please open it."

Her fingers remained closed over the little pouch. "I have yearned to have a family. But all this time, I felt certain that you loved someone else."

He got up, sat beside her, and placed one hand over his heart. "I love you, *ma chère*, only you."

Her eyes filled with tears. "But I have seen how you look at Viane."

"In the past, I have been a fool. But with all my heart, I love only you. Just think how good our life will be. Every morning, I will make espresso for you. Every evening, we will sit here under the arbor while the sun sets. Every night, I will hold you warm and close while you fall asleep. We will have a wonderful family. *Ma chère*, open it so we can begin."

One tear, and then another fell on the soft, shining silk in her hand. She shook her head.

Édouard took the little envelope, and the gold band with the glittering yellow diamond slid into his palm.

"Don't cry, *ma chère*," he said softly. He put it on her finger, where it looked exactly right.

"Please listen to me, Édouard. It is too late." Monique's lips quivered. She pulled the ring off with shaking fingers. As she held it out to him, she lifted her face to his, and it was wet with tears. "I came to tell you that I am going to marry Henri Lacoste and live in Roussillon."

Chapter Twenty-Four

Chevalier

Finally, around three o'clock in the morning, Britt fell into a deep sleep. An hour later, something awakened her. She lay still for several moments, struggling to make sense of the sound. Someone pounded on the door to the cheese shop. She pushed aside the sheet and got out of bed. Naked, she walked across the apartment, put her head out the window, and looked down.

A car idled nearby, and a man stood below her. He had just raised his fist to bang on the door again. "Wait a moment," she called. He looked up, and his hand fell to his side.

She pulled on her kimono and ran her fingers through her hair as she started down the steep stairway to the shop. "Seriously," she muttered. "What can be so important?" She stalked through the shop and flung open the door.

The man wore Bermuda shorts, a buttoned-down shirt, and tasseled loafers without socks. He held a pale linen cap in his hand. He was not much taller than Britt. In the dim light, she could not tell for sure if his eyes were green or blue, but they twinkled as he looked her up and down. He grinned, showing even, white teeth. "Sorry to wake you."

"You don't look sorry."

"I have an important package for you." An Australian accent. The car, a sporty little number with the top down, purred behind him. "You are Doctor Brittany Ann Thornton, are you not?"

"I am. Who are you?"

"I am a messenger sent by someone you know, who instructed me to impress upon you the fact that he obtained the contents of this package while acting, not in any official capacity, but as a private person." He handed her a padded mailing envelope, wished her a good day, and climbed back into the car. With a two-fingered wave, he zoomed out of the square.

Britt closed the door and leaned against it. Her hands shook as she tore the envelope open. It contained three discs, each in a slim plastic case. Heart pounding, she raced up the stairs, turned on her laptop, and started the electric kettle.

Perhaps there was a God after all.

****

Édouard winced as he swung his legs out of bed. Above the cast, his leg looked redder and more swollen than ever. And it ached. Below the cast, his toes protruded like plump purple sausages. Clinging to the handrail, he limped down the steep stone steps. He hopped across the kitchen, out the door, and another fifteen feet to the old pump. He turned up the bucket and placed it under the spigot, and then attacked the pump handle with vigor. The water from the well tasted better than the water in the house, and it was always colder. A trickle, then a stream gushed out, sparkling and splashing down into the bucket. When it was nearly full, Édouard carried it to the kitchen, dipped a cup in, and took a long drink.

He started the espresso machine and went back outside, where he settled on the steps in the early sunshine, leaned back on his elbows, and asked himself again how Monique could possibly go off and marry that fat oaf, Henri. True, Henri was a decent fellow, fair and honest. And his auto repair shop did good work. But the man had no imagination. How could she?

After she'd left the evening before, Édouard hadn't been able to sit still, so he cleaned out the barn, hobbling with one crutch, and then hoed up all the weeds between two long rows of grapevines. But no matter how hard he worked, he still felt wounded to the core. Finally, when his beautiful hen had charred to a crisp, black mummy and the new potatoes looked dry and hard, he remembered to turn the grill off. He had to throw the whole dinner in the garbage. How could she abandon him like that?

Troubadour, the black cat with the white blaze on his chest, marched across the cobbled drive from the direction of the barn, his head high, his whole bearing proud, a large mouse clamped between his teeth. His coat glistened in the sun, iridescent with health and vigor. He dropped his gift at Édouard's feet, sat beside it, and gazed up into his eyes.

"Well done, Troubadour. Thank you for not bringing it into the kitchen."

The cat climbed the steps and settled on his lap. Monique had a soft spot for Troubadour. She would miss him. As Édouard stroked the warm, silky fur, the cat settled into a steady, thrumming purr. Édouard sighed. He scowled at his foot. Finally, he got up to drink his coffee and put on his uniform.

He had barely opened the office and removed his hat when Brittany strode in. She carried a laptop in the crook of her arm. "*Bonjour*, Édouard. May I talk to you?"

"*Oui*, Brittany. *Oui*, of course." He took his seat, leaned his crutches against the wall, turned the wastebasket upside down, and propped his foot up on it.

She bent over and gazed at the bare purple toes protruding from the cast. "Your foot looks bad. How does it feel?"

It throbbed. It hurt a lot. But it did not hurt as much as his heart. "I did too much work last night and made it much worse, but it will improve again. Of that I am certain." He could not be so certain about his heart. He smiled to convince her that all was well. Her green-brown eyes met his, and he had the sense that she saw his broken heart, and he wanted to tell her what a fool he had been.

Instead, he said, "You must have something important to say to me. Something you do not wish to say while you cut for me a wedge of gorgonzola, for instance."

"I'd like to show you part of the video they filmed in the market. I want you to see Viane's expression when Jean-Luc collapsed." She set the laptop on his desk and opened it. "Two cameras were focused on her, but this one was directly on her face."

She pulled up a chair, sat down beside him, and tapped on the keys. Three times, she played a short video clip. At the edge of the frame, the blue and yellow tablecloth slid slowly off the table, taking with it the vase of flowers. Jean-Luc's gasps for air came clearly through the speaker. And Viane's face, for a brief moment, lit up in an expression of delight, clear and undeniable. Brittany froze the screen at that moment.

He said, "She looks happy. She is pleased that the video is nearly finished and the filming has gone well."

"That could be true, but I don't believe so."

"Surely, she did not realize that Jean-Luc was ill."

"You can't be sure of that. Please consider that I might be right. What if her expression means that she believes she has succeeded in poisoning him?"

"You are an amazing woman, Brittany."

"Amazing?" She lifted her eyebrows.

"*Oui*. It is amazing to me that you should suddenly appear in Chevalier and tell me that someone I have known all my life has tried to kill her husband. This is Provence. It is not America. Such things do not happen here."

"I know for certain that such things *do* happen here. I know, for instance, that she killed her own father."

"In self-defense."

"Perhaps." Her gaze did not waver.

Édouard drummed his fingers on the desk. "Even if there was a toxin in Jean-Luc's food, there is no evidence that Viane placed it there."

"You are angry that I would come and say this to you."

"This is a very serious accusation."

"And only I suspect Viane."

"*Oui. Exactement*. It is obvious to me that Viane was simply focused on her work, that she did not realize at that moment that Jean-Luc was so ill. You must admit this possibility."

Brittany gazed into his eyes for a long moment. "Perhaps you feel that you have no reason to believe a crazy American tourist."

"I do not think you are crazy." He wished he did. The worrisome thing was that she was quite sane, and she had impressive credentials. Édouard sighed. "Send me a copy, and I will forward it to Xavier, my counterpart in the Gendarmerie." He tried to keep the bitterness out of his tone. "Homicide is under their jurisdiction. I will tell him of your suspicions, but I must tell you that the gendarmes will not arrest anyone because a video showed an expression that might be construed to be unsuitable at the time."

He pushed up to his feet. "*À bientôt*, Brittany." He held out his hand. "The American way."

Chapter Twenty-Five

Chevalier

Édouard won the argument with Brittany. No question. Even though he had caved in and agreed to send the video on to Xavier. He had been firm. And clear. But he felt no satisfaction, rather, a growing discomfort with the American's insistence that Viane had tried to kill her husband.

His cat came out from under the desk, leaped onto his lap, and stared up at him. He had brought Troubadour to work today, in hopes that he would have an opportunity to charm Monique. He ran a hand down the soft black back. "You are quite right. I should discuss Brittany's accusations with Monique."

This was, of course, foolish. "But yesterday, when I went to the shop for my sandwich, she disappeared into the room where the bottles of wine are kept and would not come out." And now he understood why. He sighed. What kind of person would he be if he did not respect her wishes? "We are both hurt, Troubadour. She won't be bringing you any more chicken livers."

****

It was Britt's turn to make the sandwiches.

According to Monique, the story floating around town was that Jean-Luc had suffered a minor heart attack. And obviously, he was recovering nicely.

Things were status quo in the cute, quaint, little village of Chevalier, and everyone was happy.

Britt attacked the baguettes with a long, sharp knife, and when each sandwich was finished, jabbed a wooden pick right through it. She worked hard and fast. Monique expressed surprise at how quickly she built the pyramid in the cold case. They were ready for the lunch crowd ahead of time.

But nothing diminished Britt's feelings of frustration and impotence. Édouard was right. The video was not evidence. It proved nothing.

That day in the hospital, Dr. Brusseau talked about ordering tests for toxins in Jean-Luc's blood. But the very next day, his long-time family physician, De La Fontaine, returned from vacation, and Brusseau left for some obscure corner of Africa to work with Doctors of Mercy. When she tried to phone him, she had to leave a message, and so far, he hadn't responded. De La Fontaine, of course, refused to speak to her, citing patient privacy.

The customers tapered off in the afternoon, so she borrowed cleaning supplies from Monique's grandmother and scrubbed the old storeroom behind the shop. She emptied bucket after bucket of dirty water, hoping that if she washed and polished with all her might, she would come up with something brilliant. Finally, the room was clean, ready to serve as Arielle's office. And she was ready to admit that she could not prove Viane had poisoned Jean-Luc.

Monique wished her a pleasant evening, hung the closed sign on the door, and walked out into the square. Britt dragged her feet up the steep stairway to the apartment. She placed another call to the Doctors of

Mercy office in Paris and pleaded with them to get a message to Dr. Brusseau.

The evening stretched ahead of her, empty, and after the bustle of the day, suddenly and strangely silent. She wanted to go to Jean-Luc's farm and tell him what she suspected, but what, exactly, would she say? Britt could think of nothing that would persuade him to believe his wife had tried to kill him. It seemed more likely that she would only alienate him.

Unable to sit still, she wandered back and forth in the hot, stuffy apartment. She leaned out the window and looked down. The same four elderly women sat on the bench near the fountain, chatting as they did every evening, in soft voices, with quiet laughter. She missed Arielle, who was still in Bordeaux, teaching her happy little group of vacationers about terroir and mouth feel and the difference between single varietals and wine blends. Even one of Megan's snarky texts would have been welcome.

Britt poured a glass of rosé from the local wine co-op, sat down at the table under the window, and opened her e-mail. She discarded three messages from Rob without opening them. Then, feeling so lonely that she was about to click on her trash folder and read them, she noticed one from Oscar.

To: Brittany Ann Thornton
From: Oscar Plitman
Subject: Beijing

Brittie, I must now eat a large serving of humble pie. As you know, I am scheduled to read my paper in Beijing in September at the International Conference on Deviant Behavior. As you also know, Martin Sherwood proposed to analyze the data from my latest research and assist with the preparation of my paper if, in return, I would share the podium. It was a fair and just agreement. At this date, however, I find that he has done nothing, and will likely continue to do nothing.

About the time that you departed for gay Paree, Martin met a curvaceous, blonde femme fatale at least twenty years his junior. In her most recent employment, she performed as a burlesque dancer in Las Vegas, but injured her Achilles tendon and is now spending down the State of Nevada's unemployment compensation fund. But I digress. Judging by the fact that if I wish to speak to Martin, I must first rouse the fatuous fart from his stupor, for he now spends his days sleeping at his desk, I can only assume theatrical, athletic, and adventurous sex occupies his nights and addles what was once an astute mind.

If you have not yet determined the gist of this tale of my suffering, I am hoping that I may play upon your sympathetic nature. I implore you to return at once to Seattle, do the analysis, and write the damn paper. You are the only person in the universe I can trust to do this, indeed the only person capable of doing this given the short amount of time remaining. Please respond in the affirmative ASAP. Oscar

Britt let the idea percolate while she went down to the shop and cut a wedge of Brie to go with her wine. A month ago, even a week ago, she would have responded yes without a moment's thought. She loved analyzing and interpreting data. It was the kind of work she did best. Did she want the job? Do mice like cheese? She should pounce on this offer. It would give her career an amazing boost. And she needed to earn some money. But what about her promise to help Arielle get settled in

Chevalier? And what about Jean-Luc?

To: Oscar Plitman
From: Brittany Ann Thornton
Subject: Beijing

Oscar, you always have such nutty ideas—refreshing, but nutty. You honor me with your confidence. However, you are talking about compressing a three-month job into seven weeks. I am not certain I am that magical. And as painful as it is to speak of it, you make no mention of the pittance for which I would attempt this. Britt

He answered immediately.

To: Brittany Ann Thornton
From: Oscar Plitman
Subject: Filthy Lucre

My dear, I will pay you, in the next seven weeks, for three months' work. O.

She really needed the money. It was kind of Arielle to offer to pay her rent in return for working in the cheese shop. But Britt would have done that gladly just to help. She didn't really want to be paid. She'd feel like she was sponging off her friend.

To: Oscar Plitman
From: Brittany Ann Thornton
Subject: Beijing

Throw in the trip to Beijing and I will consider it. Britt

First, she could fly to California and have a good long talk with Megan, although that was the last thing her daughter would want. Judging by her text messages, she'd prefer to stay angry than to deal with the hurt in her heart.

To: Brittany Ann Thornton

From: Oscar Plitman
Subject: Beijing
Of course, you would share the podium in Beijing.
O.

Britt's eyes opened wide. Her heart rate quickened. She had practically begged for this a few weeks ago. And it was still the deal of a lifetime. She had to think.

Shadows straggled all the way across the square when she walked out into the balmy evening air. She called "*Bonsoir*" to the women sitting on the bench and headed down the hill to the little meadow beside the creek. Ducking under trailing willow branches, she kicked off her sandals, waded across the stream, and sat cross-legged on the cool grass.

Her phone quacked. She pulled it out of her pocket and touched the green button.

"Are you surviving?" Arielle said. "I'm so sorry I left you there by yourself. And I feel terrible for expecting you to work in the cheese shop."

"I haven't had even a minute to be bored. Seriously, it's okay." *And I'm thinking about abandoning you.* "But there's something I have to tell you before you hear about it from someone else. Remember the FBI guy in Paris? He got copies of those videos for me."

Arielle gasped. "You didn't!"

"That's not all. I showed Édouard a clip of Viane's reaction to Jean-Luc's collapse, and he sent it to the Gendarmerie."

"You went behind my back and got them. And now you've accused Viane to the homicide police."

"I had to. While he's falling to the ground, she has a totally self-satisfied smirk on her face."

"Britt, you have got to be kidding."

"I wish I were."

"So she's smiling. So what? You're reading an awful lot into a tiny moment. Seriously, Britt, I cannot believe this. I hardly know you anymore. You expect everyone to be evil."

"Not smiling. Smirking. This is my field of expertise, and it's that tiny moment that tells the truth."

"Brittany Ann Thornton, you are making me crazy." Arielle's voice trembled. It rose in pitch with each word. "I am an outsider, struggling to be accepted in that little town. Viane has boosted the economy. She's made it *the* place to be. She's practically a saint. And you are accusing her of attempted murder."

"I'm sorry, but I had to do this."

"You did not *have* to do *anything*." Arielle was practically shouting. "You are alienating a town that is not too happy about an American buying their cheese shop in the first place. They will boycott me. They will ruin my business. They will make it impossible for me to live there." Arielle hung up.

Stunned, Britt stared at her phone. She pressed the green button to call Arielle back, but it went straight to voice mail. Arielle had refused her call.

Britt crumpled into a ball and hugged her knees to her chest. She cried until her tears ran dry. After a long while, she stretched out on her back on the dew-damp grass. She tried to feel the support of the earth under her back and to believe everything would be okay. She reminded herself to breathe deeply. If only she could retreat to the time before she caught Rob with Graciella, before Thirteen and his horrid cartoons, before the FBI seized everything. Before she ever met Jean-Luc.

She heard a soft quack close beside her. A plump white duck hopped up onto her stomach and looked at her as if to say hello. It pecked at the buttons on her shirt, and after a while hopped off the other side and waddled away. She felt oddly comforted.

In the shadow of the town on the hill, evening twilight edged toward the inky black of night. With a long sigh, Britt stood and waded back across the creek.

Chapter Twenty-Six

Avignon

Britt walked out of the sleek glass train station onto the platform as the TGV to Paris pulled in. The cars glided past her, one at a time, more and more slowly.

Where would she ever get a better job than the one Oscar offered? Nowhere. No how. Not ever. Even if it only lasted seven weeks. To stand at the podium at the international conference in Beijing so soon after receiving her Ph.D. was a rare, not-to-be-sneezed-at opportunity. It would open up a world of possibilities.

All she had to do was get her bod home and dive headfirst into the data. From there, her new life would unfold. Monique and Arielle weren't the only ones beginning a fresh chapter. She was, too.

If only she'd been able to talk to Arielle and explain why she was leaving. But last night, Arielle refused to answer her phone and this morning, it went straight to voice mail. Britt sighed. Their friendship had been through rough patches before. They would get through this one, too. And Monique had agreed to stay and manage the cheese shop, so she hadn't totally abandoned her.

The train came to a complete stop. Doors hissed open. A flood of passengers came out. They meandered toward the exit, clogging the platform and brushing against Britt, making her breath come in claustrophobic gasps. Those waiting to board surged around her, murmuring, laughing, clutching bags and children, trapping her and propelling her forward with them. She planted her feet, refused to budge. One by one, they went around and ahead of her.

If only Dr. Brusseau hadn't gone off to Africa. If only she could have talked to him. If *he* were to tell her that Jean-Luc had not been poisoned, she could go home and not worry. She pressed her lips together. Stop. Stop. Stop. She had tried. She had done all she could.

Finally, only one other woman remained on the platform. The black back of her pantsuit disappeared into the dimness of the train car and, as if connected to this last passenger by an invisible thread, Britt followed. She must pray she was wrong and go on. The moment she was on board, the door sighed shut behind her, and the train glided away from the station.

At Orly airport in Paris, the ticket Oscar had promised waited for her at a customer service counter. Britt boarded a flight to London, where she would transfer to a plane to Seattle. She slid into her seat, opened her laptop, and began to sketch out a work plan. For the next couple of months, she would barely have time to sleep and eat. She would have to get the analysis and interpretation of Oscar's research done in the first four to five weeks. Then she'd begin to prepare the presentation. She needed to set up regular weekly meetings, make sure she kept him up to date and stayed on track herself.

The plane touched down, tires squelching on the tarmac, at London Heathrow. It taxied interminably, until it finally reached the terminal. As she hurried down a long corridor, watching for signs to connecting flights, her phone buzzed with messages coming in. Without pausing, she pulled it out of her purse.

The first text contained a cartoon of a woman lying on a beach with a knife sticking out of her chest. She had the same face as the others, and the caption sent chills down Britt's back.

—*Do you think she met The Unlucky Number?*—

She tapped the screen and forwarded it to Oscar.

The unlucky number. Something had changed. It was the first time Thirteen had referred to himself. Britt's heart rate picked up. Why was he reaching out to her? What if he had killed again, and he was boasting?

As if rooted, she stood in the middle of the long, wide corridor. The hustling people, the gate announcements, the stale, overheated air all disappeared. For a moment, she was alone, in silence.

She'd been irritated at Oscar for sending her to interview Thirteen that day, and with the defense of her dissertation looming, she'd been tense and distracted. If she'd really tuned in and tried harder, perhaps she could have found a way to get the kid to talk. He might have been detained and convicted. Now, if this cartoon meant he had killed another woman, her death rested partly on Britt's shoulders. She should have tried harder.

Likewise, if Jean-Luc died, even if everyone else believed Jean-Luc had suffered a fatal heart attack, deep inside, Britt would know. Her heart thudded against her ribs.

She had convinced herself that she had done all she could. But her intuition told her that the life of that beautiful man was at risk, and if he died, she would feel not only guilt, but sorrow, for the rest of her life.

She tossed her phone into her bag and ran, dodging other passengers, following signs to her airline, to their nearest customer service desk. "I have to get back to Provence right away. I have no money, only this ticket to Seattle."

Immobile, the man behind the counter stared at her over the top of his computer.

"I'm serious. I'm in trouble, and I need your help. A man's life is at stake."

"You are a doctor?" He sounded incredulous. He was buying time, wondering how best to deal with her.

Pulling herself up as tall as possible, she laid her passport and her boarding pass on the counter. "I am Dr. Brittany Ann Thornton, and a man will die if you don't help me get to Avignon right away." She could barely stand still but did her best to look stern and composed.

The agent looked at her passport, gazed at her for another long moment, then down at his computer screen. He started typing. "There's nothing to Avignon, but there is a flight to Paris Orly in half an hour. I'll see if I can get you on it."

He tapped some keys. Waited. Tapped some more. Picked up the phone and spoke into it. He heaved a sigh, took her boarding pass, let his hand hover over the printer, and finally handed her a piece of paper. "They are holding the plane at the gate." He pointed. "That way to number thirty-five. Good luck."

"You're an angel." She ran toward the large *35* that hovered above the concourse. In the jetway down to the plane, she found Stan Gibson's number at the FBI office in Paris. As she settled into her seat, she sent him a text: "Urgent. I am returning to Chevalier, will land at Orly in one hour, and I need your help."

On the ground again at Orly Airport, Britt found nothing from Stan, but Oscar had responded.

—*Thirteen AWOL for 2 days. Car stolen in Seattle abandoned in Portland. No fingerprints, but seen nearby. 2nd car stolen.*—

—*Find him. He has killed or will kill another woman who resembles his mother.*—

There was a second text message from Oscar,

—*No trace of him. But a woman has disappeared in Central Oregon, and another has been killed out on the coast, a distant cousin of Thirteen's mother. My apologies to you, Brittie. I should have listened.*—

Her intuition was right. A knot of panic rose in her chest, making it difficult to breathe. She had been right about Thirteen. She was right about Viane. And she was stranded in Paris with barely enough money for a cup of coffee. Her hands shook as she dialed Stan's cell number. "Please, please, please be there," she whispered. The ringing went on and on. Finally, she left a message and prayed for him to call her.

She scanned both her text and her e-mail messages, but there was nothing further from Oscar, and nothing from Stan. She chewed a fingernail as she read a new one from her mother, a chatty note, mostly about the weather in southern California. Then there was a PS.

—*Oh, by the way, Megan is quite excited. An older boy is giving her and Theodore, the boy next door, kite-surfing lessons.*—

An older boy? Britt's skin prickled. She would have phoned, but then Stan wouldn't have been able to reach her, and anyway, it wasn't yet morning on the West Coast, so she sent a text.

—*Do you know this older boy?*—

She was considering the art and science of hitchhiking when Stan rang. "You sneaked out of the country without telling me. Now you've sneaked back in." His voice vibrated with irritation. "I thought we had an understanding."

Britt didn't care how angry he was. "I forgot." She could breathe again. "I need your help to get me back to Chevalier. I haven't any money, and Viane Thibaudet is going to kill her husband. Soon."

"Truly." Two short syllables packed with anger and cynicism.

"Stan, I'm serious. I'd bet anything she got away with poisoning his parents. And if I don't stop her, she will get away with killing him."

"Tell me about this poison."

"Nicotine would be my guess."

"Huh. What gives you that idea?"

"When I did CPR, I tasted it, and I had some symptoms afterward that match up."

"Huh."

"Listen, she has a degree in chemistry. Distilling it would be a cakewalk. Plus, I've done some research. It's the perfect poison. There is no antidote, it passes quickly out of the bloodstream and urine, and it isn't included in normal hospital lab testing, so it could easily go undetected."

"That may all be true, but only you suspect this woman of murder. Right?"

"Monique agrees with me, and if you saw the expression on Viane's face when Jean-Luc collapsed, you would agree, too."

"Monique?"

"Monique from the cheese shop. She lives there, Stan. She sees Viane for what she is. Look, I'm telling you, the woman got away with murder."

"Murder undetected, huh?" A tinge of excitement had replaced the irritation in his voice. "You really expect me to believe that?"

"Can you really sit back and let her do it again?"

"Hold on."

There was a long pause. Britt held her breath and listened to the sound of computer keys clicking.

"Miss Marple, it would help to have proof."

Britt sucked in some air. "Definitely, Hercule. I've been trying to reach Dr. Brusseau, who admitted Jean-Luc to the hospital. He said he would order more toxicology tests. But then he went off to Africa, and I haven't been able to reach him."

"It would be even better to have proof that his parents were poisoned—if they were."

"I don't see how we can get that."

"Hold on."

Another pause. More clicking computer keys on Stan's end.

She bit her lip and waited, waited, waited.

Finally, he said, "Can you get to the Place de la Bastille?"

"Sure." She had no idea how, since she had only ten euros in her pocket. She'd beg if she had to.

"Ask someone how to take the metro."

"I can do that."

"Right. There's a tall column with a statue of somebody important on top in the middle of a huge traffic circle. You can't miss it. Get yourself over there. Stand on the south side in front of the opera."

An anxious hour and a quarter later, an old, but shiny, black sedan, indistinguishable from half the other cars in the traffic circle, darted across two lanes of traffic and halted in front of her. Stan leapt out. Ignoring the impatient honking, he took her backpack out of her hands and tossed it into the trunk, then stood with his hands on his hips and gazed at her. "I need to make this clear. I am here as a friend, on my own time. The FBI is not involved."

"Got it."

"Let's go. You look like shit, by the way. When did you last sleep or eat anything?"

The sun had set by the time they arrived in Chevalier. Stan shook Britt's shoulder. "Wake up, sleeping beauty."

"Have I been asleep?" Britt pushed her hair out of her face and looked around. He had pulled to a stop next to the fountain in the middle of the square.

Stan grinned. "You looked like you needed it. Now, before we go any further, except for your friend Monique, whose help we need, I would prefer that no one knew I came."

The cheese shop was locked, as Britt expected. While Stan parked a little way down the road, Britt went to Monique's grandparents' B&B. She walked down the hall to the back and out into the courtyard. The family sat around a table covered with flickering candles, food, and wine. Monique jumped up and hurried toward her, hands outstretched. "Brittany. Some things came for you, just an hour ago. When I told the delivery man you were not here, he said he would leave them all the same. I must show you."

Stan showed up as Monique unlocked the cheese shop, and the three of them went in. She led the way through the shop to the old storeroom. There, in the middle of the floor, were two black cases the size of carry-on bags.

They all leaned over them to read the labels: *To Dr. Brittany Thornton / From Lester F. Gras.* Britt looked at Stan. "Lester F. Gras?"

"Someone I used to know." He grinned like a kid with a cookie in his mouth and a hand in the cookie jar.

"Someone who is acting as a private person, I assume," Britt said.

"Definitely someone of that ilk," he said, supremely pleased with himself.

Monique looked from one to the other, clearly puzzled.

Stan said, "Monique, Britt says I should trust you. Can you guarantee that you will not talk about this?"

"*Oui.* If Brittany says so, then I agree."

"What is this stuff?" Britt asked.

"Are you both up for a stroll through the cemetery a little later tonight?" Stan asked.

She stared at him. "Seriously?"

"Absolutely. In the body, nicotine breaks down into cotinine. As you said, it passes quickly out of the blood and urine. However, it remains in bone and hair for a long time. So, one of these cases contains ground-penetrating radar, which will show us the skeletons in the Thibaudets' graves. The other has a machine that will drill a small hole and collect some very small samples. If they show elevated cotinine, you will have a very strong case."

"By sample, you mean a bit of the skeleton?"

"Indeed. A hair or hair follicle would be best."

Monique's eyes flashed. "May I help?"

"Yes. We need you to watch for unwanted company," Stan said.

Britt turned to Monique. "Do you understand?"

"*Oui*. Not everything, but I will help."

Stan nodded. "We should wait a couple of hours, until after midnight. In the meantime, my stomach thinks my throat has been cut. Any chance of some grub?"

"What is he saying?" Monique asked.

"He's hungry."

Britt led him into the shop. Monique opened the cheese case. "I shall make a sandwich. For you, too, Brittany."

Upstairs in the apartment, they all put on the black shirts Stan pulled out of a bag. While they waited for the village to settle for the night, Britt phoned her mother. "Mom, I need to know, who is this guy who's teaching Megan to kite-surf?"

"Honestly, Britt, I do have some judgement. I managed to raise you, after all. Besides, I told Megan she could only go if Theodore went with her."

"Theodore is a nice kid, but do you know this guy?"

"Theodore's mother met him, and he was very polite."

Chapter Twenty-Seven

Chevalier

Monique sat beside Stan, giving directions as he drove. Britt sat in the back seat, leaning forward, wanting to be close together, not wanting to miss anything. A little way out of town on the road toward the wine co-op, they passed an inn with geraniums at every window, then came almost immediately to the cemetery. A long stone wall with stately wrought-iron gates separated the tidy rows of graves from the road. Stan pulled up to the gate. While Monique and Britt climbed out of the car, he unloaded the two black cases from the trunk. "I'll go park at the hotel and walk back," he said.

Britt nodded. "Gotcha."

She and Monique each picked up a heavy, awkward case and walked through the gate. The cases bumped against their legs as they started up the slope. They stopped behind the first line of gravestones and waited for Stan. In a few minutes, he came toward them, silhouetted by moonlight.

Monique led the way uphill, winding between the silent granite sentinels that marked the earliest graves, to the white marble headstones inscribed *Gaspard Thibaudet* and *Martine Thibaudet*. All three stood quietly for a moment, heads bowed in apology to the dead, and then Monique slipped back down toward the gate to keep watch.

Stan snapped open the locks on one of the cases. He lifted out a black device about the size of a box for a pair of cowboy boots. "State of the art ground penetrating radar." He sounded like a proud kid with a new toy. He pressed a switch, and the top of the instrument turned faintly green and glowed like a computer screen. Holding it over the grave of Jean-Luc's father, he moved it slowly back and forth until white shapes started to show up. He held it still for several seconds. The shadows brightened and came into focus. Britt gasped. They were gazing at the bones of an arm and shoulder.

"Holy shit," she whispered. "It's like looking at an X-ray."

Stan chuckled. "Like magic." He stepped toward the headstone, centered the machine, and found the skull. "Okay, hold this right here."

Britt held it as still as she could. In her hands, the pebbly surface felt warm. It was heavy, and the image fluttered each time she moved, even if she drew a deep breath.

Stan snapped together a tripod and set it under the device. "We need it to be steady." He took it from her and rested it on the tripod. He tapped a small keypad beside the screen a few times, peered at the screen, and then gave a thumbs up. "Perfect."

Monique appeared, coming up the hill, a silhouette in the moonlight, moving from grave to grave toward them. "Jean-Luc's truck stopped by the gate." Monique's voice was barely audible.

Stan said softly, "I'll record the GPS coordinates.

We can come right back."

"Quick, he's coming this way," Monique whispered.

Each of the women grabbed a case. Stan picked up the machine, tripod and all. Stooping low, moving from one gravestone to the next, they slipped farther up the hill to a line of umbrella pines, then sank down on the grass, each behind a tree, to wait. Britt mentally thanked Stan for the black shirts they wore. Jean-Luc went to his parents' graves. He stood for several minutes and then moved off to the left a short distance. There he knelt and stayed still for a long time. "His first wife's grave," Monique whispered.

Almost an hour passed before he made his way back to the gate. Finally, Britt heard his truck start and drive away. It was two-thirty a.m.

Back at the Thibaudet graves, Stan repositioned the radar and sharpened the focus on the skull. Monique went back down toward the road and disappeared in the shadows near the gate.

Stan opened the second case and removed what appeared to be a long tube with a cable protruding from one end. He attached the cable to the radar machine, then positioned the end of the tube over the skull. "There's a drill inside, with a small-bore core sampler. I can guide it right to the skull, and we should get a nice sample of bone, and with luck, some hair follicles."

A low buzz told Britt it was working. Stan scrutinized the screen. "It's down 1.2354 meters." The noise stopped. A few seconds later, he removed a small cylinder from an opening on the side of the tube. "Sample number one," he said, handing it to her. "I can do three samples of each grave. There's a marking pen in the case. Put the name and a number on each one." As the buzzing sound started again, Britt labeled the first sample *Gaspard Thibaudet 1*.

Fifteen minutes later, she labeled the last one *Martine Thibaudet 3*. Stan put the equipment away, then clapped Britt on the shoulder. "Let's get out of here."

The trio piled into his old black car, and they all began to jabber, congratulating themselves and each other, but grew quiet again as Stan drove up the deserted, silent street. He parked in the shadows near Viane's restaurant, and together they walked across the square to the cheese shop.

Near the fountain, they stopped to read a sandwich-board sign advertising a fundraiser for the church roof, a buffet dinner. Catered by Viane. All proceeds to the church. Tomorrow evening. Britt's heart rate quickened. The perfect opportunity for Viane.

By the time they collapsed in the little apartment above the cheese shop, the first pink light of dawn shone in the eastern sky. Without turning on any lights, Monique opened a bottle of champagne.

"I will take the samples to the lab," Stan said. "I will instruct them to send the results to Lester F. Gras, care of the cheese shop. You should get them in two or three days. With a little luck, you will have proof of elevated levels of cotinine in their skeletons." He paused. In the dim light, Britt felt, rather than saw, his gaze resting on her face. "Or not."

He lifted his glass, as if in a toast. "If what you suspect is true, you will have to figure out what you're going to say to the gendarmes when they ask how you got it."

Britt grinned. "I'll say I got it from the FBI."

Stan laughed. "Touché."

He stretched out on the floor and immediately began to snore. Monique tiptoed out. Britt lay down on Arielle's bed and tried to sleep. When Stan left for Paris a couple of hours later, her eyes were still wide open. There was only one thing left to do.

Chapter Twenty-Eight

Chevalier

"Get a grip," Britt muttered at the mirror. "I have to do this." She smoothed makeup over the dark circles under her eyes. If what she believed was true, then unless she could stop her, Viane would kill Jean-Luc that very evening.

Her fingers shook. If Viane had poisoned the senior Thibaudets, it was no accident that she had gotten away with it. She had brains, guts, determination, and no sense of guilt or remorse.

What if Viane laughed her off? That would be the smartest thing to do. But then what? She had not come up with plan B. Therefore, Plan A had to work. She settled Arielle's wide-brimmed black hat on her head and slid on a pair of big dark glasses, then descended the steep stairs from the apartment. She walked through the cheese shop and stepped out into bright morning sunshine. It was still early, but already it was hot, and although she had just showered, sweat trickled down her back. With determined steps, she crossed the square to the restaurant and climbed the stairs.

The door was locked, but she could see Viane at the desk in the little foyer, arranging flowers in a vase—lilies in hot orange and yellow colors. Britt rapped on the glass and looked away so that her face

179

was hidden by the hat. The door opened, and she turned. "Good morning," she said, removing her sunglasses.

Viane stiffened. "*Bonjour*." Her tone was frosty.

Britt said, "I'm sure this is a busy day for you, but it is important, very important, that I talk to you."

"I don't understand."

Now that she had begun, Britt felt calm. The jitters were gone. "I believe we could be helpful to each other. Extremely helpful." She inclined her head toward the open door to the kitchen, where a young man in a white apron stood, peeling onions. "Where can we talk privately?"

The other woman stared at her for a long moment, then led the way to a table on the terrace but did not sit down. "We are alone. And you are correct. I am very busy." She leaned over the table and swiped away a speck of dust. "What is this about?"

"It's very simple. Last month, I discovered that my husband is a criminal. He was arrested for fraud. He lost our home, all our money, and all our belongings. So, you see, I have nothing. I am here as Arielle's guest, or I would not have even a single croissant for breakfast."

Viane's posture relaxed. "I am sorry for you, but why have you come to me? Are you asking for a job?" Her eyebrows arched above her dark brown eyes. "Are you a cook, perhaps?"

Doing her best to look friendly and hopeful, Britt leaned in and said, "What I have in mind pays much better than cooking."

"*Mon dieu*, I should like to know what that is. Pray tell me."

Britt took a step closer. "First, tell me what happened to Jean-Luc's parents."

Viane backed away. "They died." She placed a hand on her throat, then quickly put it down at her side.

"Did you poison them?"

"They were old." Her eyes narrowed and fastened on Britt, like a cat watching a bird just beyond her reach.

"I am a psychologist. In fact, I am an expert on criminal behavior, and I have reason to believe that you poisoned the Thibaudets."

The woman's hands went to her hips. She scowled. "*Vraiment!* Truly! You were there? You observed this?"

"No." Britt waited a beat. "But I was there when you tried to kill your husband."

Her eyes widened with surprise, then her brows drew down in anger. The color rose in her cheeks, and her respiration rate picked up.

Bingo. Britt had her. Time to reel her in. "Don't worry." She sat down and pointed at the chair on the opposite side of the table.

Viane perched on the edge of the seat. A look of steely cold determination came over her.

Britt folded her hands and rested them on the table, then leaned in with what she hoped was a conspiratorial smile. "If you will help me start a new life, I will keep your secret safe."

Viane tipped back her head and gazed at the sky for a moment. Then she glared at Britt, her eyes hard and angry. "That is a ridiculous idea." Her lips curled in a sneer.

"I admire your style."

"I think your problems have led you to become unbalanced."

"I've narrowed the poisons you might have used to three, but I'm betting that you chose nicotine."

Alarm flitted across Viane's features. Her brows went up, and her eyes got big. She put a hand on her mouth, then quickly removed it.

Britt smiled. "So simple to do, especially for someone like you, with your chemistry degree. Elegant really. And it would be easy to mitigate or disguise the side effects."

"That is ridiculous." Viane stood and leaned across the table. "Who will believe you?"

Britt got slowly to her feet and bent forward, until their faces were only inches apart. Very softly, she said, "I believe I can convince the Gendarmerie to investigate your husband's parents' graves, that they will find traces of cotinine in their remains. I'm sure you know that it's a metabolite of nicotine. It will not have passed out of their bodies before they died, and a significant amount would indicate nicotine poisoning. I shall speak to them today, unless, of course, you would like to help me with a small sum of money."

Viane jerked back.

Britt stood as tall as she could and gazed down at her opponent. "I shall also tell them that Jean-Luc may collapse at the church dinner tonight, and if he does, they will find a high level of cotinine in his blood. In fact, they may be able to find abnormal amounts in his hair from your previous attempt."

"Greedy American bitch."

"I'm not greedy. Listen, it's simple." She shrugged, lifting her palms. "My silence is worth a lot to you. I do not ask for much. Just enough for a new start. In return, I will not tell a single soul what you have done. However, if you are not interested..." She started toward the lobby.

Viane moved to block her path. "I cannot allow you to go about telling these lies to others."

"Then it is fortunate that I need some money right now. It seems a happy coincidence, *n'est-ce pas?*"

Viane pressed her lips together.

"I have written everything down and sent it to a safe place. If anything happens to me, it will be opened and read by someone who will make sure that you are exposed."

"I must have time to think of how to help you."

Britt moved closer, right into her personal space. "You don't have time, and you don't have options. If you don't have the cash, you need to give me a promise, in writing, today, that you will pay me."

Viane stalked into the tiny lobby, pivoted, and placed her back against the door in the entry. Her cheeks were bright above her starched white jacket. "I will close for the afternoon at thirty minutes after two. If you return at that time, I will have my chef prepare lunch for both of us." She lifted her chin. "We can discuss your wages at that time, as professionals."

"*D'accord.*" Britt held out her hand. As expected, Viane ignored it. With a sneer, she turned and yanked the door open.

Out in the hot Provençal morning, Britt resisted the urge to look back over her shoulder and forced herself to walk with slow, measured steps. Her heart was still beating triple time, but she had accomplished what she set out to do. Viane wouldn't dare poison Jean-Luc tonight, and as soon as she gave her some money or a promissory note, she'd have evidence to take to the police.

But why did she say she needed time? Highly unlikely that she was going to go get a bucket of euros. More likely, she was scheming right now to poison Britt's lunch. Did she keep a supply of poison at the restaurant? Probably not. That would be dangerous, so she would have to go somewhere and get some. Possible? Possible. A definite maybe.

Resisting the urge to run, to get as far away from Chevalier as possible, she slipped into the cheese shop to get the keys, then strolled down the road to the garage where Arielle's little red sports car waited. She slid in and started the engine. It was still early. She'd be back in time to open the shop.

In a couple of minutes, Viane's sedan glided by. Britt waited until two more vehicles passed, then, wishing Arielle's car weren't so conspicuous, nosed out into the street. What if she was only going to the wine cooperative to pick up today's supply of wine?

At the bottom of the hill, the green sedan turned toward the farm. Another car slotted in between them, and they all picked up speed. Twelve minutes later, Viane turned in at the Thibaudet farm. As Britt drove on by, she could see that she had parked near the barn, but there were no trees along the road to cover her, so she couldn't stop and watch. Best to act as if everything was normal. Go open the cheese shop.

Chapter Twenty-Nine

Chevalier

By two-thirty, Viane's starched white jacket felt damp and limp. She stood under the whirring air conditioner in the kitchen and drank from a large bottle of ice water. She'd arrived back at the restaurant minutes after Gascon, the other chef, gashed his hand with the boning knife. She had applied pressure, but he clearly needed stitches, so off he went, and she had done most of the cooking herself. Pierre, the *sous chef*, had stepped right up to help with the lunch rush.

But now the kitchen was a mess, and she still had to deal with that *garce d'amerique* before she could start preparations for the church dinner. No worries. She would handle it.

"Pierre, go now. I will finish up."

"Certain?"

"*Absolument*. Go."

Pierre shucked his jacket and dropped it in the hamper in the back corner by the stairway to the cellar. He ducked his shaved head out the door. The servers, too, had finished with lunch customers, and the cashier. "Come back one hour before the church buffet," she told them all. "Now it is hot, and you are all tired. Go. Rest for this evening."

Barely one moment after the last one departed,

Arielle McGregor's friend came in. How a class act like Arielle got teamed up with her, Viane had no idea. She reminded herself to smile, then stepped past her and locked the door. "Come to the kitchen. My chef cut his hand, so I shall prepare our lunch."

"I would prefer to talk about our business."

"So American. So uncivilized. You may help. That way, you will know that what I offer you is not poison, *n'est-ce pas?*" In the kitchen, she yanked off her tall white hat, opened the buttons at the top of her jacket, and rolled back the sleeves.

The stupid bitch went to the sink and began to wash her hands. "If we are to do business, then of course I will help."

She did have a certain style. Her smart black dress could only have been found in Paris, and her hair had been cut by an expert. It made her eyes look bright and minimized her nose. Yes, a good cut. And a lovely color. Actually, she made a worthy opponent. Getting rid of the *garce* would be a pleasure.

Viane released her hair from the clip that held it up, shook her head, and allowed her curls to cascade freely. "We shall make a *salade niçoise*, but first, a glass of rosé. It's perfectly chilled." She chose two glasses from the wine rack, set them on the stainless-steel counter, and brought a carafe of wine from the refrigerator.

She smiled again as the carafe hovered over the glasses. "You see? I will drink the same."

"*D'accord.*"

She poured a glass and took a long sip. "*Voila!*" She poured another for her guest, handed it to her, and clicked the glasses together. "To working with you." They both drank. Viane allowed herself a small smirk

186

of satisfaction.

She might as well enjoy this moment. "Salads are made here, on this side of the kitchen." She wiped a shiny stainless-steel counter with a white towel, tossed it in the sink, and set two plates down. "All the vegetables we need are in the bins along the back. If you would place lettuce on these plates, then I will add tuna and vegetables." She liked people to die happy, with wine and good food in front of them. It was her one regret that she had not cooked for her own father.

She took another long drink of the wine. She loved the floral bouquet, and it felt good to hold its coolness in her mouth. Brittany sipped hers, then set it down carefully, as if guarding her glass. Viane almost laughed aloud. She was beginning to like her. Too bad they couldn't be friends.

Brittany made a bed of Bibb lettuce leaves on one of the gold-rimmed plates. The delicate green color and the deep wrinkles in the leaves always delighted Viane, and today she thought they looked especially pretty. "We must talk about your strange idea that I tried to kill my husband and his parents. Whom have you spoken with about this?"

Brittany turned and rested one hip against the counter. She lifted her glass and drank. "Only you." Her eyes were wide and innocent. "Why would I tell anyone else? It would no longer be a secret. And only a secret is worth the price I ask."

"And if I am not interested in your offer, then you will go to the Gendarmerie with this bizarre tale?"

"I will."

"What proof will you offer? Even if my husband's parents were exhumed and toxin was found, no one could say how it got there."

"Can you afford to take that chance?"

"Of course. I have done nothing wrong." Viane topped up their glasses. "However, an investigation would cause me much distress. By accusing me, you would harm my business, and not only mine, but my husband's as well. In fact, you would bring harm to all of Chevalier."

She shrugged her shoulders, held up both palms, curled her lips down, an expression of confusion and distress. "I may decide to help you, but not because of what you think. Because we are both women. Sisters. *N'est-ce pas?*"

****

Britt laid crinkly green lettuce leaves on the second plate. Civilized. Of course. They would be civilized. She had expected the woman to be anxious, irritated, or both. The girlfriend demeanor, the breezy, chummy, "let's make lunch together" threw her off balance.

Viane stood right beside her, elbows touching. As she reached for tomatoes and green beans, she nudged Britt farther along the counter. A quick glance around told her that she had been maneuvered into a corner of the kitchen with no exit, only an old wooden trap door that swung up from the floor and leaned against the wall. It was not far from where she stood. Her heart beat a little faster as she went to it and peered downward.

Far below, a bare lightbulb cast a weak glow on a long flight of stone steps that had been carved right out of the hillside. The steps were high, uneven, and worn from years of use. The cool, dank, musty smell of damp earth wafted up to her. "Everything else in the restaurant is new. This cellar is the only thing that has not been brought into the twenty-first century," she said. "Why?"

"Because I like it. Perhaps you would like to see?" Viane smiled, a wide, generous smile.

Britt shrugged, shook her head, smiled back. Her head felt light. Her eyes were slightly out of focus. It was the wine. She had been too nervous to eat breakfast and was running on way too little sleep.

Viane said, "It is the perfect place to store wine."

The wine tasted so good. It was cool in Britt's parched mouth. And it made her feel as if she was floating. Maybe she was a little euphoric.

"Besides, it is historical. During the war, Madame Goddard, who owned this building, hid many Jewish families down there and helped them escape over the Pyrenees to Spain. When the door is closed, a cupboard can be pulled over it, and the cellar is hidden. Even now, few people know it exists."

Britt took a deep breath. A person could hide a body down there, hers, for instance. The weird thing was, the idea made her want to giggle. She must focus. She turned back to the salad bar. "You are amazing. You have put this town on the map. Everyone says so."

"This town is nothing, I tell you, nothing. To the tourists, it's provincial, quaint, and so very endearing. They come to stare and take photos of us, the noble French peasants.

"Everyone works and works and works and never has anything. On market day, they count their meager monies from the sale of the vegetables and olives they have grown, and it is a pittance. After days and days of hard labor. And they are grateful. For what, I ask you? I shall go to Paris. I shall have Michelin stars. The best people will come."

Britt had to force herself to concentrate. "I believe you could do that." She gathered her scattered thoughts. "Unless I tell the police what you have done. I am not asking for much, just a small amount to go back to the United States and find a place to live. That is all."

Viane's hands stopped working. "Americans," she said in a voice laced with derision. "This is not a dirty street corner in New York." The tongs with which she held bright green beans stayed suspended over one of the plates. She glared. "If you tell a crazy fantasy that I have tried to kill my husband, you will be scorned." She plunked the beans onto the plate beside a little heap of red potatoes.

Britt nodded. "You're right. I will be thought a very silly woman if I tell everyone what I suspect." She was having a hard time remembering why it was so important. She took in a deep breath. "But when you try again to kill Jean-Luc, they will remember." That was it. "Do you want to take that chance?"

Her hostess grinned. She selected a handful of tiny tomatoes and held out her hand. "Try this. You will never taste anything better." Then she popped one in her mouth.

As their eyes met, Britt took one. "To you, and your culinary secrets." Immediately, a strange taste, the same as the taste of Jean-Luc when she performed CPR, flooded her mouth. Her lips felt numb. She spit the tomato into her hand.

When she looked up again, Viane held a heavy, long-handled pan. Like a baseball bat, she swung it back over her shoulder.

Britt saw the round copper bottom coming toward her. She ducked and put up her arm, but she was too late. The pan clipped the side of her head. She stumbled backward toward the cellar steps. The other woman grabbed her shoulder and gave a mighty shove. She crashed against the trap door, fell, and landed on the top stair.

Viane kicked her hard, then got down and pushed with both hands. She tumbled down, bouncing off the hard, stone edges. Her arm broke with a loud crack. Her neck snapped back, and her head hit. About halfway down, she stopped, head down, her shoulders against the wall, and one leg hanging off the stairway. It hurt too much to breathe.

Viane's feet clattered after her, and when Britt opened her eyes, she crouched on the step above. Even in the meager light, a smile clearly lit her face. A smug, self-satisfied, happy smirk. "So unfortunate. You had such a terrible fall on these old, historic steps."

Britt wriggled closer to the wall, away from the edge. Her ribs screamed. She eased the leg that dangled over the edge up onto the stair, gritting her teeth against the pain that shot from her hip all the way down to her toes. Her neck hurt like holy heck, and her head ached as if it would split open. She didn't dare look at her arm. She could feel the bone protruding from it.

Viane moved to crouch beside her. "You'd like to know how I did it, wouldn't you?" she crooned.

Her image swirled in and out. Britt forced her eyes to remain open. Oddly enough, except that it was so hard to breathe, she didn't really mind the pain. "You think I care?" Her voice croaked. "Look, all I want is a little money."

"Since you're going to die anyway, I'll tell you."

Britt's anxiety drifted away. She felt no sense of panic. "I know you are extremely clever."

"Did you know there's enough nicotine in a single cigarette to kill a man?"

"Everyone knows that," Britt jeered.

"But you have to know how to extract it and concentrate it." Viane sounded injured, defensive.

"You're lying." Britt's voice seemed to be coming from somewhere else. Seriously, it was a huge joke. "Nicotine makes you sick. Nausea and vomiting are the first symptoms. Jean-Luc did not vomit. He collapsed, just like his parents."

Viane laughed. "That's true. Do you think I wanted their vomit? Do you think I want your vomit all over my stairs?" She chuckled. "I put an anti-nausea, anti-emetic medication in your wine, and a little heroin, to make you happy. You are happy, aren't you? In mine too, of course. It won't hurt me. But you—soon after I inject the nicotine, you will stop breathing." Something glinted in her hand, a syringe.

"And after a while, you will call for help because a stupid American fell down the stairs."

"*Oui*. After I eat our salad." She squinted at the syringe, pointed the needle upward. "I'm sorry we couldn't be friends. It would be nice to know someone who understands." She grasped Britt's arm, pinched up her muscles near the shoulder. "You will just feel a little sting."

Alarm cut through the fog in Britt's brain. She wrenched away, made a fist, and punched her on the nose.

Her arms flailed the air. The syringe flew out of her

hand. She teetered on the edge of the stair for a long moment.

Bracing her back against the wall, Britt shoved with both feet.

Viane shrieked as she pitched over and fell to the floor below.

There was a thud, a long moan, and then silence. Britt slumped back. With each breath, sharp pain tore at her chest. Struggling to her knees, she turned around and crawled to the bottom, holding her broken arm against her chest.

The light from the one bare bulb shone on the woman, who lay without moving, her hair flung out from her face like a halo. Britt knelt beside her and found a strong, steady pulse. Viane rolled her head from side to side. Britt struggled to her feet. As she turned toward the stair, she glimpsed a small, shiny, cylindrical object on the floor. She bent and scooped up the syringe.

Viane groaned. She started to sit up.

Cradling her broken arm, not looking at the jagged bit of bone sticking out below her elbow, one tortured step at a time, Britt made her way back to the stairs. She peered at Viane, who had fallen back and lay without moving. Dizzy, breathing in shallow gulps of air, she slumped to her knees and began to drag herself from one step to the next. Halfway up, she put her head down and rested. When she opened her eyes again, Viane was on her feet, reeling drunkenly.

Britt urged herself on. In the kitchen, she pulled herself up to stand beside the counter, then limped to the lobby with the happy yellow and orange bouquet. Behind her, she heard labored breathing.

In slow motion, Britt turned the lock, flung open the door, and walked outside. Holding her breath against the pain, she staggered down the steps and into the square. She was almost at the fountain in the middle when from what seemed a terribly long distance she heard Monique calling her name.

Her knees buckled, and everything went black.

Chapter Thirty

Chevalier

Deep in Édouard's heart, a spark of hope kindled. Because the first moment there was trouble, Monique cried out for him. She called his name so loudly that he heard it all the way inside his office. He came, hobbling as fast as he could on his crutches, glad, almost giddy with joy, because when she needed help, he was the one she relied on.

With tears in her eyes and blood on her pristine white apron, she knelt beside Brittany, who lay in the hot sunshine near the fountain. "Get the medics, Édouard. Please. And you must find Viane."

He knew it was unwise, even foolish, to hope she would break her engagement to Henri Lacoste. But he so wished she would. While he telephoned for help, Édouard fanned the spark in his heart until a tiny flame took hold. Maybe she didn't really love Henri. Maybe she would change her mind, stay in Chevalier. And he would ask her again to marry him.

In his haste to do what Monique asked, he stumbled on the steps leading up to Viane's restaurant and came down hard on his broken foot. Pain shrieked up his leg, doubling him over. He paused, gulped down a wave of nausea, then hustled on up, past the cash register in the foyer, and into the kitchen.

Viane, her thick black curls in disarray, crawled toward him. Grasping the salad counter, she pulled herself up to stand. Blood gushed from her nose. One side of her face had swollen until her eye was merely a slit. She grabbed a large, sharp knife. "Where is she?" she yelled, swinging the knife wildly in the air.

Édouard dropped his crutches and clamped a hand around her wrist, squeezed, and removed the knife from her hand. Then, still holding onto her, he snatched a towel from the counter and handed it to her. "Press this to your nose."

She tossed the towel aside, sucked in a giant breath, and yelled, "That whore. She pushed me down the stairs." She took a step and screamed with pain. Her head snapped back, and she tumbled to the floor.

He noticed, as he again phoned for medics, that for the first time in his life he did not feel sorry for her.

By evening, he had questioned most of the shopkeepers and employees on the square. No one had seen anything until Brittany stumbled down the steps from Viane's restaurant and Monique ran to help her. He was interviewing the waiter at the café next to the cheese shop when he received a phone call from the hospital. Viane was awake and out of recovery, the broken pieces of her hip pinned to a metal plate. Brittany was still asleep from the anesthesia needed to treat her injuries.

Édouard suspected that Brittany had confronted Viane and accused her of poisoning Jean-Luc, like the crusader she was. Right or wrong, she stuck to her principles. He had to respect her for that.

The question was, what happened next? He needed the facts. Just the facts. That was going to be a problem.

It seemed that only the two of them knew. Without doubt, each of them would have her own perspective, her own story, and neither might be exactly the truth.

Viane was holding an ice pack to the side of her face and shouting at the nurses when he arrived at her hospital room.

He would have preferred to be anywhere else. His stomach growled, and he was thirsty. He hadn't had even a moment to elevate his foot, so it had swollen up again inside the cast, and it throbbed with each beat of his heart.

But that was nothing. He had a growing sense that he had allowed his regard for Viane to blind him, and that made his gut churn. He wished he had listened to Brittany when she came to his office, that he had taken her seriously. If it turned out that she was right, then the blame for whatever had happened today rested on his shoulders.

He could not run from this. He settled into a hard, straight-backed chair beside Viane's hospital bed. His mind must be clear and unbiased. Opening his notebook, he took out his pen. "I need you to tell me what happened, from the beginning."

"Édouard, my friend, so formal." She looked away, wiped a tear from her eye, and then turned a watery smile in his direction. "How can you be so cold?"

Weary, stilted, and annoyed with himself, he replied, "I have to do my job, as you know." Unless he undid the harm he'd allowed to happen, he feared he would still feel this way when he was old. "Now, please, tell me what happened."

"That woman is *complètement folle*." Viane's voice quavered. "She came to my restaurant. She said she wanted money."

Édouard kept his expression neutral. "Madame Thornton came to the restaurant and asked for money."

"*Oui*. She tried to blackmail me. Imagine. I laughed at her, in her face, as such an idiotic idea deserved. I said I would not pay. I told her, 'Ask anyone. They will tell you I have made Chevalier what it is. Why would I try to poison my husband?' I tell you, Édouard, she is dangerous. I have never known anyone to be so angry. She pushed me to make me fall down the stairs. I swear by the Holy Mother, she almost killed me, and I believe that was her intention.

"I tried to save myself by holding onto her arm, and she fell together with me. When I woke up, I was on the floor in the cellar, and she was gone. I crawled up the steps with my broken hip—all the pain—and then, my dear old friend, you came to help me."

"If she tried to kill you, I must report this to the Gendarmerie. They will come and investigate, and it will be out of my hands. So, I must ask you, are you certain that was her intent? Could it have been an accident?" He braced himself for a tirade.

She turned her face away. In the past, he would have stumbled all over himself, told her whatever she wanted to hear, said whatever it took to soothe her. But this time, he just waited.

After a long pause, she said, "That woman is spreading lies, and you don't believe me. What type of person are you? How can you question me like that?" Tears ran down her face. "We have been friends since our childhood."

No matter what he said, she refused to speak another word. Instead, she rang for the nurse, who helped her put the head of the bed down. Then she closed her eyes and lay still.

He knew very well that she would not budge. There was only one thing he could do to improve the way the evening was going—satisfy his stomach. He went in search of a hearty serving of cassoulet.

By the time he had eaten dinner and returned, Viane had told her story to everyone who attended her, and the hospital buzzed with it. Édouard could imagine the rumors spreading outward in ever-widening circles, like the ripples in a pond when a stone is dropped in, all the way to Chevalier and beyond. He knocked, then stepped into her room.

Jean-Luc sat beside the bed. He stood and greeted Édouard with his normal courtesy. Viane, on the other hand, merely glared at him.

"I'm sorry that you've been hurt, Viane," Édouard said, "but I must ask you again to tell me, from the beginning, every word, every detail of what happened between you and Madame Thornton, leaving nothing out. Please."

"You are not my friend." Her voice sounded cold, hard, angry. She turned to Jean-Luc. "You see? He doesn't care."

Jean-Luc took her hand. "Édouard is just doing his job. He cannot express any type of preference."

"I already told him. He didn't believe me." She rang for the nurse.

Édouard said, "I need to hear more, much more, and I will not judge."

She closed her eyes. Jean-Luc began to pace back and forth in the tiny room, his brow wrinkled. The nurse came in, and Viane said, "This policeman is upsetting me, and I need to sleep."

"I will go." Édouard started for the door. "But tomorrow I shall return. You will have to talk about this, whether you wish to do so or not."

By then, Brittany had come out of surgery. The orthopedist had repaired the compound fracture in her arm and taped three broken ribs, and because she had possible internal injuries, she had been sedated. The doctor was adamant. Nobody would be allowed to talk to her until she had further examinations the next day.

With a long sigh, Édouard started for home. If only he hadn't been such a fool, Monique would be waiting for him. She would pour him a glass of wine, and they would talk over all that had happened.

Not tonight. No. It would not be the same. But she would want to hear about Brittany. Again, that tiny spark of hope fluttered in his heart.

Chapter Thirty-One

Avignon

Early in the morning, before preparing for market day, Jean-Luc drove to the hospital, accelerating and braking gently so as not to spill the bouquet of white daisies and blue cornflowers he had picked.

He stood at the side of Viane's hospital bed. As she repeated her story, she clung to his hand, as he'd so often wished she would. Perhaps something good would come of this ordeal. Perhaps she would realize how good a life they could have. "Surely Madame Thornton did not intend to push you down the stairs."

Viane gazed into his eyes. "I swear to you, my darling, she did." She shook her head. "That poor, deranged woman."

Jean-Luc's back stiffened. Deranged? *Non*. Brittany was not deranged. His feet shuffled. He felt himself shift emotionally away from Viane, and that brought a tiny, anxious knot to his chest, but he could not shift back.

"She told me her husband is a liar and a thief. I imagine that this is dreadful for her. I would have liked to help her. But she threatened to spread a dreadful story that I tried to poison you."

Had Viane tried to poison him? Jean-Luc bit his tongue. What kind of a husband would he be to ask such a question? Instead, he said, "Everyone knows that is not true."

But the question Dr. Brusseau had asked him, when he lay in this same hospital, had kept him awake last night. Now, again, it perturbed him. Did he think it strange that both of his parents and he, himself, had collapsed without previous symptoms? And all the doctor's questions about what he had eaten. Jean-Luc took his hand away from hers.

Viane continued, "When I refused to pay her, I could see in her face that she wanted to kill me. I tell you, my dear, we must be on guard against her. She is exactly like one of those dangerous dogs, sweet on the surface, but nasty inside."

As his wife's voice droned on, Jean-Luc's attention strayed to that morning at the market when he happened to glance up and see Brittany sitting at the café. She had looked alone and weary, but patient, like a flower bud waiting for the kiss of a sunbeam, ready to open and bloom and share its fragrance. When he drove his truck to the parking, he walked back the long way in order to pass by her table. He felt compelled to speak to her. And then, when he took the pencil from her hand to correct her sketch, their fingers touched as briefly and lightly as a butterfly kiss. A frisson of electricity shot between them, and all the sounds and sights of the market, the whole world, in fact, melted away until only the two of them stood on the planet. For a few beats, the windows of their souls opened to each other. From the startled expression on her face, he knew she felt it too.

The memory was as clear and sharp as if it had just happened, and he wanted to keep it that way. If he accepted Viane's story, it would taste bitter. He would lose something valuable. He sighed.

Viane stared at him as if waiting for a response. He clasped her hand. "Perhaps what has happened is a gift from God. You have wanted to leave, to be in Paris."

She frowned.

He hurried on. "Perhaps now you will stay in Chevalier. We could truly be a family, *n'est-ce pas?*"

She pushed the button to make the head of the bed go down. "I am tired now. You must excuse me." She let go of his hand and closed her eyes.

His words sounded foolish, even to his own ears. After a few minutes, he tiptoed out of the room. He wished he thought she had had a change of heart, that she would settle and be happy in Chevalier. But she was, after all, Viane.

He should just accept her account of yesterday's events. But he wanted to know what Brittany would say. He would go now and talk to her. But at the door to her room, he hesitated. She would almost certainly deny that she pushed Viane down the stairs.

It would be one against the other. And he had promised, when they married, to protect and support his wife. He walked on down the hall, past the visitor information desk, and out into the fresh morning air. He must get ready to go the market.

****

Britt tried to understand.

A woman's voice, quiet, speaking French.

Then a man's voice, speaking English. If she concentrated, she could understand. "Brittany, the doctor is asking how many fingers she's holding up."

Frowning, Britt opened her eyes and looked. "Fingers. Many fingers." Her tongue felt thick and heavy. It stuck to the roof of her mouth.

The woman's voice again. Then Édouard. Édouard's voice, translating. "Wiggle your toes."

Britt's toes were far, far away. She didn't know if they wiggled.

Again, he translated. "Squeeze my hand."

She felt a warm, dry palm. She could. She knew she could.

"I'm going to look in your eyes with my light."

A bright light. It hurt her. She closed her eyes. Gentle fingers lifted one lid and the light shone in again. Then the other lid.

Something hard tapped her elbow, and her arm jerked. Then her knee.

****

Britt floated in a warm, soft place. In the mud bath? No, not that. The mud bath had smelled of lavender and lemon. Instead, there was an astringent, antiseptic odor in the air. Soft-soled shoes strode past, with quick, important steps. Voices murmured. A light blanket covered her. Where was she? A square patch of sunlight fell on the wall opposite. Nearby, someone was yelling, a woman. Screeching. In French. Britt listened, but it took too much effort to try to understand. She closed her eyes and floated a while longer.

"Brittany, Brittany." A man's voice. Édouard. She turned her head toward him. He was sitting beside her bed. She frowned. "What time is it?"

"It's almost noon, and the doctor says I may talk to you now." He opened a notebook. "Can you tell me what happened?"

Viane. The cellar stairs. Britt's heart started to pound. That was why her ribs were bound and her arm had a cast from shoulder to hand.

"Monique said you came out of Viane's restaurant and collapsed beside the fountain in the square."

Her struggle to get outside, to get to safety, where there were other people. "When?"

"Yesterday. What do you remember?"

The day Viane would try again to murder Jean-Luc if she didn't stop her. The fog in Britt's brain began to clear. "First, tell me, where is Viane now?"

"Here in the hospital. In the next room, in fact."

"Ah, good." Britt relaxed back against her pillows. "Then Jean-Luc is okay."

"*Oui*." Édouard looked as if he had more to say, but only shook his head. "Jean-Luc is well."

Britt pressed the button to raise the head of the bed, so she could see him without twisting her neck. Then she told him everything. How the wine made her head spin so that against her better judgement, she tasted the tomato Viane offered and immediately recognized the same taste as Jean-Luc's mouth when she did CPR. How Viane hit her with the pan and pushed her down the stairs, then bragged about killing Jean-Luc's parents and tried to inject her with nicotine. And how she shoved Viane, causing her to fall. From time to time, she paused, and Édouard helped her hold a cup with a bent straw, and she took a long, cool drink of water.

Finally, he sat back in the chair. "If what you say is true, it is my fault that you have been injured, and I am sorry." He rubbed a hand across his forehead. "Even if it is not what happened, when you told me what you suspected, I avoided my responsibility to investigate."

"You didn't want to believe that anything this sinister could happen in your village."

"*Merci*, Brittany, but that does not excuse me. At once, I shall convey what you have told me to my counterpart in the Gendarmerie. His name is Xavier, and he will work with me to discover the truth." He got to his feet and gazed at her for a long moment. "If you, if anyone, ever again tells me something like this, I shall listen."

After he left, Britt drifted in and out of sleep until long, slender fingers closed around her hand. "Dear God in the morning, Britt, what the effing hell have you been up to?"

This was as close to saying the f-word as Arielle ever came. Britt's eyes popped open.

Arielle leaned over the side of the bed, peering at her, her forehead wrinkled in concern. "I can't leave you alone for even a minute."

Britt squeezed her hand. "I hope it's not you who's been yelling."

"Viane. She's screaming at everyone. Apparently, her coffee is cold, or something equally horrible is happening to her." Arielle bit her lip. "I'm sorry I didn't believe you."

"No worries. It's okay." Britt grinned. "I love you anyway."

"The rumor flying around Chevalier is that you tried to blackmail Viane. I know you're a little crazy." Arielle winked. "But not that nuts."

"Actually, I did."

Arielle's eyebrows shot up. "Seriously?"

"Seriously. I hoped if I could get hush money from her it would be tantamount to an admission of guilt, something I could take to the gendarmes."

"That's brilliant. So, now the whole town thinks

you pushed her down the stairs because she refused to pay you."

"They're wrong. I didn't push her. I kicked her."

"Brittany Ann Thornton, where are your manners?"

Britt allowed herself a small smirk of satisfaction. "It's okay. She pushed me first. After she drugged me with heroin and hit me with a ginormous frying pan. Then she was going to finish me off with a syringe full of nicotine." Britt's hand flew to her mouth. "I forgot about the syringe. I had it in my hand."

Chapter Thirty-Two

Chevalier and Avignon

At the market, the entire population of Chevalier and the surrounding countryside hovered around Jean-Luc's stall. If they had been as intent on buying his products as they were on quizzing him about Viane, he would have made a good profit.

He deflected the curiosity of casual acquaintances by keeping up a patter about how he had perfected his process for his newest cheese, a variation of Emmentaler. He cut generous cubes of it from his first large wheel and offered them on the tip of his long, sharp knife.

It was harder with his friends. They would sidle up to him when the crowd tapered off and say quietly, "Eh, old man, what about Viane?"

Each time, a little stab of doubt shot through his chest and made it hard to breathe. "She had a bad fall but will recover soon," he said, over and over again, ignoring the real question. Then, as quickly as he could without offending, he turned to the next customer. His friends nodded knowingly as they drifted away.

Normally, he loved market day. Normally, it invigorated him. But today, it drained every drop of energy out of him. He was glad to fold the large green umbrella, pack up the truck, and drive away.

When he returned to the hospital in the late afternoon, a gendarme stood in the corridor, beside the door to his wife's room. Alarm bells went off in his head. The Gendarmerie handled homicides.

Viane sat in a chair beside the bed, her broken leg propped up, her arms crossed on her chest.

Jean-Luc tipped his head toward the door. "Why is he here?"

She glared at him. "I'm not stupid enough to talk to you or to him. I'm waiting for my lawyer."

"You have telephoned for Didier?"

She tossed her head. "Your friend Didier knows nothing. Why would I call him?"

Suddenly, it was too much. Jean-Luc glared back. "That is very rude, Viane. I have spent this entire day acting and speaking in support of you. Didier is a good friend, and I must tell you that I am beginning to think you do not deserve my loyalty or the help of kind, intelligent folks like him."

He stalked from the room and out of the hospital, into the hot Provençal sun.

Perhaps he should listen to Jacqueline. Get a divorce. Find someone who wanted to be with him, with the two of them. He walked through the parking lot and down the street until he came to a café where he saw no one he recognized. Alone at last, he sat at a table in the shade of a plane tree and ordered a beer. It came, cool and nicely hopped. As he drank, he began to regret his outburst.

Viane did not tolerate stress well. She never had. He should not expect it now. Divorce? *Non.* From his childhood, his parents had taught him, and he had believed, that marriage was a sacred vow, not to be broken. He would not go down that path. He needed to be strong and steady when his wife was not.

He went back to the hospital, intending to sit beside her. But Marcel showed up in one of those skinny black suits that hugged his ass and made his legs look like stove pipes. With him came a short, dumpy, bald man wearing a similar suit—on him, a fashion nightmare. Escort and battleship, they sailed into Viane's room ahead of Jean-Luc.

Marcel introduced the man, who carried a bulging leather briefcase, as a leading litigator from Paris. Monsieur Pascal would straighten things out, *bien sur*. Pascal shook hands all around and declared himself *enchanté* to make their acquaintances. Jean-Luc felt as if all the air had been vacuumed out of the room.

The lawyer sent everyone away. The door closed behind them, and with a quivering knot of doubt in his gut, Jean-Luc began to pace the corridor.

Pascal remained with Viane for an hour and a half, and finally, at the doctor's insistence, left. After Jean-Luc helped her back into bed, she leaned against the pillows and closed her eyes. He pulled the blanket up over her. "*Ma chère*," he said softly, "you have had a trying day."

Her eyes snapped open. Her face contorted with such venom that he took a step back. "This is your fault," she shrieked. It hit him like a physical blow.

Pivoting on one heel, he marched next door to Brittany's room. He would get to the bottom of this now. Brittany was sitting up in bed, alone. One arm, propped up on pillows, had a cast from shoulder to hand. Her face had turned into one puffy purple bruise. He sucked in a breath. He would not have recognized her. She beckoned him to come in, and with concern in her voice, asked if he was well.

He stoked his anger as he walked to her bedside, determined not to feel sorry for her. "*Oui*. I am well."

"I am so glad."

It pained him to see that one side of her mouth was too swollen to smile, and that she had difficulty forming her words. Part of him wanted to reach out, to touch her, to comfort her.

She said, "I have been worried about you."

He crossed his arms on his chest. "My doctor has diagnosed that I had only a small heart attack, so why do you accuse my wife?"

"I am very sorry." She gazed into his eyes. "But I find it difficult to believe that both of your parents collapsed exactly the way you did, in front of a group of people. And I believe you were all eating food prepared by Viane."

Still gazing at him, she paused.

"Yes." What else could he say?

"It's unlikely to be a coincidence that this happened to all three of you."

He opened his mouth to speak, but she held up her hand and continued, "It is possible that you were poisoned. I beg you to be very careful about what you eat. Please. Prepare your own food and drinks."

The blood rushed to his face, but he kept his voice even. "Poison? *Non, non, non*, Brittany, how can you say such a thing?"

"Yesterday, when Viane thought I would die, she told me she poisoned your parents." She raised her hand again, palm out, forestalling his response. "Perhaps she was not telling the truth, but I believe she was."

He pressed his lips together and shook his head. "*Non*. That cannot be. *Non*. I felt suddenly that I could not breathe. But *c'est tout*. That is all. My parents—" He shrugged. "My parents, yes, they became suddenly ill, as I did. But my father died of a heart defect. My mother died of grief. Dr. de la Fontaine has diagnosed this. I did not die. It is simply that my heart stopped, as my doctor has told me." He tried to smile but his face felt stiff, frozen. "You see? Each of us is different."

"In my job, I study the behavior of people who commit crimes, including people who commit murder." She held his gaze. "I understand this is difficult to accept, but I believe I am correct. And if I am correct, then she may try again. I beg you, please, do not eat food she has prepared."

Jean-Luc's fists clenched. "I do not believe you." He stepped back, away from the bed. "In America, you are not loyal to your spouses. You discard marriages as if they had no meaning. You litter your cities and towns with abandoned marriages, exactly the way you litter your roads with abandoned beer cans."

His voice had risen. He was shouting, and he couldn't stop. "This is not America. We do not behave this way in Provence. In all of France, we do not behave with such disregard. When we say we shall love and honor our spouse, we do so. When I married Viane, I gave my solemn word that I would cherish and protect her. Every day, I do so. I will clear my wife's name of this terrible insult you bring against her.

"You insult me, you insult the town of Chevalier and Provence, indeed you insult all of France."

Body trembling, he strode out of the room and down the hall toward the exit.

Chapter Thirty-Three

Avignon

Jean-Luc's angry outburst cut Britt to the core. She knew it meant he was afraid. Afraid she was right. Afraid Viane had betrayed his trust and indeed poisoned him. But no matter how she tried to console herself, it hurt. A lot. She wished she could pull the sheet over her head and disappear.

When Arielle arrived a short time later, Britt still felt too raw to talk about it. Fortunately, she didn't have to. In fact, she barely had to talk at all.

Arielle was bursting with news. She pulled a manicure set out of her purse and set to work on Britt's fingernails. "Guess what? Dominique, the jeweler, says Édouard asked Monique to marry him, but she said no."

"Aha! That's why she hides out in the wine room every time he comes into the shop."

"Yup. But listen to this: This morning, she told me she broke her engagement to her high-school sweetheart, some guy named Henri Lacoste, so she's not going to move to Roussillon after all."

"You've got to be kidding."

Arielle's grip tightened. "Hold still. No kidding."

"Is she still avoiding Édouard?"

"She was. Until this morning. There were some little black turds on the floor behind the cheese case, so when he came for his sandwich, Monique asked if he would bring his cat. Édouard wouldn't have looked happier if he'd won the lottery. He went right home and scooped up Troubadour, and what a handsome fellow he is, too, in his shiny black coat.

"In less than a minute, Troubadour flushed out a rat, which ran out into the square and hid under that stone ledge around the fountain. Troubadour went right after him. He hunched down under the ledge and swatted at it with his paws. And something very interesting rolled out." She paused and gazed at Britt.

Britt scowled. Arielle would make her crazy yet.

"I'll give you a clue. It was something round and shiny."

"The syringe? Troubadour found the syringe?"

"Yup. You must have dropped it when you fainted, and it rolled under there. Anyway, Édouard gathered it up in his handkerchief and took it away."

"You could have told me right away. I've been worried to death that I dropped it in the kitchen and Viane got it back."

Grinning, Arielle opened a bottle of fire-engine red nail polish. "I wanted to brighten up your day."

"So that's why the police came and took my fingerprints."

"Probably. And that's not all. Before Troubadour finally nailed the rat, he pulled out a bunch of old dried leaves and a shriveled-up red pepper."

"Holy cow. I'd forgotten the pepper."

"Édouard has it now."

****

Viane's case was looking good, according to Pascal, the attorney. "First of all, there is no proof that you tried to poison your husband. None. And Fontaine is standing by his diagnosis.

"As for the idea that you poisoned Jean-Luc's parents, when you told Madame Thornton you had done so, you were being sarcastic, were you not?"

"Of course."

Pascal nodded. "I will argue that it was a case of gallows humor. You responded to a tense, dangerous situation with an attempt to de-escalate the conflict." The lawyer reiterated this several times, to the point that Viane could repeat it without looking away, blinking, or touching her hand to her mouth. These behaviors, he said, could make her look as if she were lying.

Then he went on, "In the unlikely event that the Gendarmerie were to take this allegation seriously, they would have to exhume the bodies. Then, even if they found that your husband's parents had been poisoned, they would have no way to link you with such a crime. So, there is no point in doing this."

Viane wished Pascal would finish and get out of her room. His slow, pedantic manner of speech annoyed her. "Of course there isn't."

"I am more concerned about the syringe Madame Thornton claims to have taken. We must try to find it."

"My mother is coming back from Spain. She will arrive today and immediately begin to search for it."

"Excellent. I believe the police have already questioned your employees and searched the garbage, but so far, it appears to be missing."

"It is most likely in the cellar under a basket of vegetables."

"If no one can produce it, then it was a lie, a story

trumped up by Madame Thornton. In the meantime, allow the police to take your fingerprints. There is nothing to be gained by refusing, and it will look better if you cooperate."

"Is that all?"

"If all goes well, the only issue will be which of you assaulted the other. It will be your word against hers. Don't worry about that," he said, as he stuffed his notes into his briefcase. "That's easy."

****

Britt's phone quacked like a duck. "Brusseau" flashed onto the screen. There *was* a God. Britt picked it up.

"*Je suis désolé*, Madame Thornton," Dr. Brusseau said. "I am sorry not to talk to you before, but I am stationed in a remote village. Only today I came to a larger town and received your messages."

"Do you remember me? I was with Jean-Luc Thibaudet in his hospital room a few days ago."

"Yes, certainly. M. Thibaudet gave me permission to discuss his case with you. How may I help?"

"Did you diagnose a heart attack?"

"*Non.*" He sounded surprised. "No, I did not."

"But after you left, Dr. de la Fontaine said he had a heart attack. Apparently, that was his final diagnosis."

"Truly?"

"Yes. You said you planned to have further tests done, to see if he ingested something poisonous."

"Please excuse me, Madame. I must attempt to discover what happened."

Without another word, he rang off, and Britt was left staring at a silent phone.

****

Viane hated the all-white room with its antiseptic smell. She glowered at Jean-Luc's bouquet of daisies and cornflowers, then plucked them out of the vase. When he was in the hospital, she'd ordered a huge, lovely bouquet to brighten his room, and in return, he'd gone out to the garden and picked this scrawny handful of flowers that grew like weeds. About to toss them in the wastebasket, she hesitated, then stuck them back in the water. Pascal, the attorney, had been emphatic. She must behave in every way as part of a devoted, loving couple. This would be her best defense.

Loving couple—ha! If her husband loved her, he would have helped her buy the *Cochon Qui Rit*. Now, not only had he refused to assist her, he had crushed her last hope of raising the money. He had contacted Gustave and Gunther Mueller, the sausage makers, and told them that his patent was not for sale. If she could get her hands around Jean-Luc's neck, she'd wring it.

She would have to beg *Cochon's* sellers to return the money she had pledged. It was her entire savings, and under the terms of the contract, they were entitled to keep it. She could only hope that out of the goodness of their hearts, they would give it back. If they didn't, she wouldn't even be able to pay the film crew for her next podcast, or, for that matter, Marcel. Of course, Marcel was no fool. Even now, he was living in the mansion in Paris, doing what he did best—looking out for Marcel.

****

Coming into his office, Édouard glanced at the phone on the corner of his desk. The message light blinked rapidly. He picked it up, pressed a button, and a male voice came on. "Dr. Brusseau here. I must advise you that I disagree with the discharge diagnosis made by Dr. de la Fontaine in the case of Jean-Luc Thibaudet. Apparently, he did not find the results of my physical examination and the results of the tests that I ordered.

"Jean-Luc Thibaudet did not suffer a heart attack. Of this I am certain. His heart is strong and healthy. I have ordered the laboratory to release the results of certain tests to you. They show elevated levels of cotinine, the substance resulting from the metabolism of nicotine, in Monsieur Thibaudet's blood. It may be of interest to note that his blood also contained a small amount of heroin and an anti-emetic medication. These latter substances would mask the symptoms of nicotine poisoning. If the ingestion of these substances was not intentional on his part, then the residuals in his blood suggest a clever attempt of murder."

Édouard sank into his chair. Evidence was beginning to pile up. He could no longer pretend, even to himself, that Viane hadn't tried to kill Jean-Luc.

"My telephone access is intermittent," Brusseau continued. "If you wish to speak to me, please leave me a message, and be available to talk to me on Wednesdays or Fridays between the hours of noon and four pm. *Au revoir.*"

For the second time that day, Édouard phoned Xavier, his counterpart at the Gendarmerie. Viane's strategy had been brilliant, of course. Who would suspect her of poisoning Jean-Luc while making a video in front of a crowd? No one.

Except Brittany Thornton.

Chapter Thirty-Four

Chevalier

Jean-Luc walked out of the hospital into the warm evening air. It had taken a lot of energy to deflect the sly remarks from his friends at the market that morning and even more to forgive Viane's hateful outburst. But that was not all.

He wished, more than anything in the world, that he had not shouted at Brittany, that he had not blamed her for the turmoil in his soul. The woman who saved his life when he collapsed in the market, the woman— he couldn't think about that right now. Why? Why had he yelled at her? His shoulders bowed under the gravity of the day.

He shrank from the answer. If Brittany was right, if Viane murdered his parents, it was his fault. They had worked hard all their lives. They deserved a long, happy old age. But if she was right, he had robbed them of that by bringing Viane into their home.

He had robbed them of watching Jacqueline grow up, and her of their love. He had robbed himself of their company and of the everyday joys of life well lived. If she was right, he would never forgive himself. Pray God she was mistaken. Well intentioned, but mistaken.

He squeezed his eyes shut and pinched the bridge of his nose, hoping to stop a raging headache.

That bright morning in the market, when he first saw her, she laid siege to and captured a corner of his heart. It seemed eons ago, and now that little corner felt bruised and battered. He vented a long sigh.

When he reached his truck in the parking lot, he opened the doors to let out the heat, went and stood in the long shadow of a plane tree, and turned on his phone. A voice message from Jacqueline waited. She had stayed home today with her grandparents, Marie-Claire's parents, because of a cold.

Although she still sounded sick, her raspy, breathless voice did seem better. "Papa, I must show you something." She went on at length, insisting that he hurry home. No doubt she had found new litter of kittens in the barn. In spite of everything, he smiled.

He started the truck and rolled down the windows and headed toward Chevalier. In the stillness of the valley, the evening air, smelling of newly mown hay, flowed around him. He tried to enjoy it as he normally did, but all he could see was Viane's red-faced glare.

With childish candor, Jacqueline had pointed out to him more than once that Viane was not the person he tried so hard to believe in. However, that didn't mean she had tried to poison him or, God help him, his parents.

He sat back and relaxed his grip on the steering wheel. He must not despair. Just as the rapids that churn the mighty Rhone in the spring subside with the advent of summer and allow the river to resume its peaceful, meandering course, so these turbulent times would pass, and peace would come again.

As if guided and pulled by a tractor beam, he turned in at Didier Delacroix's farm. They had gone to school together. Then Didier went to university in Toulouse but kept in touch. When he emerged an attorney with offers of jobs that would make him a lot of money, he returned to Chevalier, to a quiet practice and a small farm in the valley. The city, he said, was no place to raise a family.

Jean-Luc found him in his cherry orchard, a short walk down a grassy path from the barn. Didier handed him a basket, and as they both picked warm, sweet cherries, Jean-Luc told him everything.

At last, Didier broke in. "Could it be that Brittany is right?"

"In my heart, I cannot believe it, but how am I to know, my friend?"

"It's complicated. *Bien sur.*" Didier picked cherries and waited.

Jean-Luc felt grateful for his silence. That was the thing about men. You could think. They would not pummel you with questions. They would not push for answers. "Why are women so hard to understand?"

"Ah, the mysteries of the opposite sex."

****

As Jean-Luc drove into the garage behind his cheese-making room, the sun was sliding down over the roof of the barn and setting a wispy, low-lying bank of clouds aflame.

He followed the path across the field to the small fieldstone house where Marie-Claire, his first wife, had grown up and where her parents still lived. Jacqueline had fallen asleep in the living room. He laid his palm on her forehead, checking for a fever. Her eyes opened, and she sat right up.

"Papa, I have been waiting all day for you."

"Here I am, *ma petite*." He sat beside her on the edge of the soft, worn, leather sofa. "What is it you wanted to tell me?"

"*Show* you, Papa. I must *show* you something."

"It is late now. Why don't you show me in the morning?"

"Papa, it is important. I *told* you." She sat up, slid her feet into her sandals, and headed for the door. "I found it when I was playing with the kittens in the top of the barn." She kissed her grandparents, promised to feel better tomorrow, and marched ahead of Jean-Luc along the path. When they reached the barn and stepped inside, Jean-Luc put his hand on her shoulder and waited until his eyes adjusted to the dim light. Moist, warm, cow smells enveloped him. He heard the whicker of his saddle horse, and from somewhere in the row of cows, a thump against the side of a stall.

Jacqueline picked up a flashlight at the bottom of the stairway leading to the loft and turned it on. He followed her up, treading softly, so as not to disturb the animals. At the top, the mound of hay was so high he couldn't see over it. But beyond the hay, another light reflected off the rafters. He switched Jacqueline's off, pushed her behind him, and crept closer.

Wham. The sound echoed off the ceiling. A guttural voice muttered. *Wham.* Side by side, Jean-Luc and Jacqueline crawled to the top of the haystack, then lifted their heads and peered over.

At the far end of the loft, a thick oak door led to the room where his grandparents had hidden downed British aviators and members of the resistance during World War Two. A torch lay on the floor, pointing at the door. Térèse Stephanopolous, Viane's mother, grunted as she swung an axe at it. *Wham.*

Jacqueline pressed her face against his ear and whispered, "She came today in her caravan and parked it under the trees in the pasture, like always. She can't open that door because I have the key." Jacqueline pulled a skeleton key out of the pocket in her shorts and held it up for him to see, then put it back.

Viane's mother swung again. The wood splintered around the lock.

"There's chemistry stuff in there. That's what I want to show you."

Térèse picked up the light and shone it on the door. Then she slid her hand through the hole. They heard a click, and she went into the narrow, windowless room.

"I heard what Madame Thornton said," Jacqueline whispered. "I think that is where Viane makes the poison."

Jean-Luc felt the blood drain out of his face. He lay there for a full minute. It was true, then. He shook himself. He must act. He slid back down, stole around the haystack, and stood outside the room, looking in. A shelf ran along one wall. Glass jars and beakers and tubes of various sizes stood on the shelf. There was a burner connected to a tank of compressed gas. The woman stooped to place a beaker in a large straw basket, which sat at her feet.

"Good evening, Térèse."

She whirled to look at him.

Jacqueline sidled up to press against him. "See?"

"This is mine, I tell you." Térèse turned back to her task.

Jacqueline snorted. "Then why don't you have the key?" She dangled it in front of her.

The old woman's wrinkled brown face contorted in anger. She glared, pointed a crooked finger at her, and spoke rapidly in an incomprehensible dialect. Then, in French she said, "I have placed a curse on you. You will be dead before your next birthday."

Jacqueline gasped, clutched a handful of Jean-Luc's shirt, and pressed against him.

He put his arm around her. "Do not worry. It is nonsense. Pay no attention." He hugged her tight. "Go, *ma petite*. Tell your *grand-mère* and *grand-père* they must find M. Chevalier and tell him to come." He spread his feet wide and placed one hand on each side of the doorframe. "Térèse and I will wait."

****

The next morning, Jean-Luc rose early. In the stillness of the new day, he drove to the cemetery. With the warmth of the early sun on his back, he knelt on the wet, soft grass, and for a long time, he neither thought nor spoke. As keenly as when he watched Marie-Claire's coffin disappear into the rich, dark earth, he felt his heart break. Losing her hurt today as much as it had when she closed her eyes and whispered, "*Je t'aime*" the very last time.

Viane had never taken Marie-Claire's place. Viane didn't know or care who he was. He had told himself, over and over, that he had everything a man needed. But today, he must admit that he had been lying to himself. His wife cared for no one but herself. He had chosen to ignore this fact, to live under the pretense that their marriage suited him. In truth, if she had her way, she would consume all that was his, all that had been Marie-Claire's, all that would rightfully belong someday to Jacqueline. He whispered a prayer, then stood and strode out of the cemetery.

He went straight to Didier.

"What brings you to see me today?" Didier asked, his eyes on Jean-Luc's face, and Jean-Luc felt naked, as if his friend knew very well why he had come.

They sat in the office, a book-lined room at the front of the house, each with a cigar and a glass of pastis. Didier booted up the computer on his battered-but-tidy oak desk and composed a new will. The terms were simple. If Jean-Luc were to die or become incapacitated, Marie Claire's parents would be Jacqueline's guardians and would hold in trust all his goods and properties until she came of age.

"My friend," Didier said when the will was finished, "I advise you to file for divorce at once. Do it today."

"*Oui*, I must do so, but there is one more thing. I have negotiated to buy a restaurant in Paris for Viane. It was to be a surprise for her birthday."

Chapter Thirty-Five

Avignon

Every inch of Britt's battered body hurt like holy heck, but she woke up in the morning feeling grateful. Her intuition was spot on. She had interpreted Viane's behavior correctly. And she was braver than she had ever suspected. So what if she was starting a whole new life with nothing? It wasn't scary anymore. It was going to be just fine.

She made it all the way across the room to the bathroom by herself, and back into bed, too.

By the time Édouard came to see her, she could smell chicken broth and hear the clatter of lunch trays on a cart in the hall. He had news. "The syringe Troubadour found under the fountain had both your fingerprints and Viane's on it, and the lab analysis shows it contained concentrated nicotine. So did the dried-up red pepper."

He was quiet for several moments, gazing at the floor and twisting his hat in his hands. Then he said, "Obviously, this validates your suspicions. Therefore, Xavier, my counterpart in the Gendarmerie, arrested Viane a few minutes ago."

"What will happen to her?"

"She remains in her hospital room with a guard. After she is discharged, she will be held in jail."

Britt felt a genuine twinge of regret. "I'm sorry. Such a beautiful, talented woman. Such a waste."

Édouard tucked his hat under one arm. He stood straight and tall. "It is difficult for me to accept."

"Of course. She is a lifelong friend."

He bowed his head. "*Oui*." Then his pale blue eyes met hers. "However, there is little doubt. You have saved Jean-Luc's life. I thank you for that. And I wish with all my heart I had considered what you told me much more carefully."

****

News of Viane's arrest spread more rapidly than measles, and when Arielle arrived after lunch, she was bursting with the bits of gossip eddying around Chevalier.

Britt's phone chimed, signaling a text coming in from Megan.

Arielle stopped jabbering and glanced at the screen as she handed it to her. "What would that little night owl be doing up so early? It's barely morning over there."

Britt tapped the screen. "She says it's the best time of day for kite surfing. Oh, and the boy who is teaching her wants to send a photo." She scrolled down. Her breath caught in her throat. "Omigod. No. No. No."

"What's wrong? You've gone totally white."

"It's Thirteen. The kid who killed his mother." She gripped the phone so hard her knuckles blanched. "He has his arm around Megan. Damn Oscar. Damn everybody else who examined him. Damn all those idiots who let him go."

Arielle stared, her eyes wide in alarm. "Holy shit."

Britt swung her legs over the side of the bed. "I've

got to go."

"Okay, okay. Let's think about this. How are you going to get on an airplane and go to California? You're on an IV, and you can barely walk down the hall."

"I can yank out this damn IV."

"Let's call the police."

"No police. It's me he wants."

"The cops are trained to deal with this."

"If they interfere, he will harm her. I have to go."

"Tell Oscar. He can help you figure out how to handle this."

"I'm going. If I don't show up, he will hurt her. That's what this means."

"Okay. Okay. I believe you. You know what you're talking about. But you are not going alone. I'm going, too." Arielle closed the door to the room. "Look, I'll work on getting us there. But it's a long way. It will take hours. Please, call Oscar. Trust him. He will know what to do. Maybe he can solve this before we get there."

Oscar's phone went straight to voice mail, and she had to leave a message.

A tense hour later, Monique arrived with a large leather tote bag. "Your passports and the things you asked for are in here," she said. "I also put in a bottle of acetaminophen and printed your boarding passes."

With one quick yank, Britt pulled the IV out of her arm. "Acetaminophen," Arielle said, as she helped her into a skirt and blouse. "That's all you're going to have for pain."

"I don't care. Let's go." Monique fashioned a sling out of a scarf to support the cast, and Britt slid her feet into the sandals Arielle held for her.

Arielle paused at the door. "They may have arrested Viane, but you're still under investigation for assault, you know, and a guard is standing right out there in the corridor. Better wait a minute." She headed out into the hallway.

Monique draped a shawl over Britt's head and pulled it forward, hiding the bruises on her face. She beckoned to Britt, and they peeked out.

Arielle had sauntered a short distance past the guard. The man turned to face her, his back to the door. She was chatting quietly in French, and even without looking, Britt knew she was smiling that smile that made men melt into puddles of goo.

Shaking and short of breath, Britt clung to Monique's arm. They slipped out of the room and turned the opposite direction. Arielle would keep him distracted all day if necessary, but she did her best to hurry. Monique peered at her. "Okay?" she asked quietly.

They turned a corner. A man wearing the same uniform as the guard approached them. He was only a few feet away. Britt bowed her head and shuffled forward, hoping to be taken for an old woman. The man returned Monique's soft "*Bonjour, Monsieur*," and then they were alone. Thirty more feet, twenty, ten. The exit doors slid open, and the stifling afternoon air, full of exhaust fumes and dust, blasted against them. It was hard to breathe.

A wooden bench stood nearby. Britt collapsed onto it. The seat felt burning hot through the fabric of her skirt, but it was better than standing.

Monique set the leather bag beside her. "Rest here. I shall bring the car."

As she drove up and stopped at the curb, Arielle stepped out of the hospital. "We did it. Come on. You are out of here." She helped Britt into the front seat and climbed into the back.

Fifteen minutes later, they stopped in front of "Departures" at the airport, and they all got out. "I shall pray for your safety," Monique said as she kissed Britt, first one cheek and then the other. "And for your health."

Arielle already had both passports, along with their boarding passes, in one hand. She slung the tote bag over her shoulder. "I checked us in online. It's not far to security." She peered anxiously at Britt. "We're a little late, but I know you can do this."

"Try to stop me." Britt followed her into the cool interior, glad to be out of the heat, relieved to be on her way. "I will text Megan. Thirteen won't harm her if he knows I'm on the way."

"As soon as we get to the gate."

"He won't hurt her. It's me he wants." She repeated it like a mantra on the short flight to the Charles de Gaulle Airport in Paris.

At de Gaulle, Arielle arranged for an electric cart. They climbed on board, and it lumbered off through hurrying hordes of people. Britt's broken arm, her ribs, her legs, and her whole back ached. Everything hurt. She closed her eyes and gripped the edge of the seat with her good hand.

At the gate, boarding for Los Angeles was just beginning. Arielle helped Britt to the front of the line. Their passes were scanned, and Britt limped down the jetway, hanging onto Arielle's arm. Halfway to the plane, a man in a black suit came from behind and stopped her. "Madame Thornton, you must return to airport security."

Britt's breath caught in her throat. "I can't miss this flight. My daughter's life is at risk."

The man shook his head. "*Désolé*, Madame." His dark brown eyes looked sorrowful. "Perhaps if you come quickly."

Arielle spoke in rapid French. His response came so fast, Britt couldn't understand.

Arielle turned to her. "Britt, they're serious. You're a material witness to Viane's attempt to murder Jean-Luc. They will put you in jail if they must in order to keep you here."

Britt's knees buckled, and she would have fallen, but the man scooped her up as easily as if she weighed nothing. An attendant standing by the door of the aircraft grabbed a transport chair and brought it to them. The man gently set her down in it. "*Désolé*, Madame," he said again. He began to push the chair back up the ramp.

"How about Stan?" Arielle pulled Britt's phone out of the tote bag and handed it to her.

She tapped the screen. A text popped up, a cartoon of a girl with a noose around her neck and a note:

—*Doctor Britt, I've got your lovely daughter. She is having fun and feeling fine. So far.*—

She wanted to cry.

The man pushed the transport chair back to the gate, where the throng of passengers surged around them, trying to get closer to the front of the line. Then they were past the gate and headed down the concourse.

Britt's hand shook so hard that Arielle had to find Stan's number for her. After six rings, it went to voice mail, and she had to leave a message. Desperate, she dialed Oscar's number again. They passed the next gate, and the next, then entered a small, square, off-white room without windows. Here, just as Oscar answered, she lost connectivity. She struggled to her feet and started back to the corridor.

The man blocked the doorway. "You must wait here, Madame."

Arielle took Britt's phone. "Look, I'll tell Oscar. And I'll try again to get Stan." She went out, and the man closed the door.

Britt watched the minutes tick away. How much time did she have? How long did it take to get all the passengers on board a 747? What would happen if she couldn't get to Megan?

Arielle opened the door and would have stepped back inside, but the man shook his head and motioned for her to leave, then blocked the doorway.

Ignoring him, Arielle peered around him. "I called Stan—" He shut the door again.

Britt limped over and yanked it open. "I have done nothing wrong. Let me go."

"You must *attendez*, Madame. *Désolé*."

She couldn't see Arielle. She couldn't overpower this muscular giant filling the doorway. Her heart thudding against her ribs, she returned to the chair and sat down. The only thing left to do was to pray, and she hadn't done that since her father died.

At last, a gray-haired woman wearing a border patrol uniform marched briskly into the room, followed by Arielle. "Madame Thornton, I regret this delay. The Gendarmerie is anxious that you remain in France for questioning in the case regarding Viane Thibaudet."

Britt held her breath.

"However, I have received a most unusual guarantee." She peered at Britt over the top of her spectacles. "This has never before happened. The FBI, and therefore your embassy, assures your return." She took Britt's passport and boarding pass, perused them, and handed them back. "I shall take you to your gate."

The second Britt and Arielle sank into their seats, the doors to the airplane closed and the flight attendants started the preflight checklist.

Britt's phone buzzed with a text from Stan:

—*This is not what I meant when I told you to stay in touch.*—

The phone buzzed again, with another note from Stan.

—*Nevertheless, I congratulate you. The results of your graveyard caper are in. The samples from both of the senior Thibaudets show elevated cotinine. I have used the name of Lester F. Gras to inform Monsieur Édouard Chevalier.*—

Britt closed her eyes, let the tears flow down her cheeks, and prayed.

Chapter Thirty-Six

Southern California

Eleven and a half hours after lifting off in Paris, the plane touched down at Los Angeles International. Britt scanned her phone. Nothing. It was 7:40 p.m., and she hadn't received a text or e-mail from her mother, Megan, Oscar, or anyone. Why?

She closed her eyes. Inhale, two, three. Exhale, two, three, four. Thirteen knew she was on her way, and as long as he was waiting for her to show up, he would not harm Megan. She was the one he wanted. Not Megan. Inhale, two, three.

Finally, the plane taxied up to the gate and stopped. Britt glared at the seat belt sign, willing it to go off. It was still glowing when a flight attendant leaned down and said, "Please come with me." He picked up their leather tote bag and led them to the door. It opened as they approached.

A short, stocky, uniformed officer waited in the jetway. "This way, ladies."

Britt grabbed his arm. "What is going on?"

The officer put his hand over hers and gave it a little pat, then held it for a moment. "I've been asked to accompany you to the helipad."

"Helipad?"

"That's all I can tell you. Come. The sooner we get

there, the better."

Arielle put an arm around her shoulders and urged her forward. Britt limped up the ramp, doing her best to hurry—toward what? Something terrible had happened. The worst. They were waiting to tell her privately and in person.

An electric cart stood at the top, and the three of them climbed on. Britt rebooted her phone. She prayed, but when it came back up, she still had no new messages.

The cart lumbered along the concourse, its shrill beep grating on her nerves, past an intersection teeming with people and ringed with cafés and bookstores. After interminable gates and concessions, they stopped at a set of doors with a keypad at the entrance. The driver entered a code. The doors swung open. He turned off the warning beep and drove down a long corridor, alone and quiet.

But there were still no messages. Nothing. Britt closed her eyes and prayed. At the end, an elevator took them to ground level, and they drove out onto the tarmac to a large black helicopter. The pilot sat at the controls.

A man in an anonymous black suit stood beside it. He helped her down from the cart. "Doctor Thornton, I'm Special Agent Branson."

She could barely hear him over the sound of the engine. If he expected her to be polite, it was just too much. "I don't care who you are. I don't care if you're God himself. Where is Megan?"

"Ma'am?"

Arielle tossed the tote bag in the chopper and whirled back to face him. "What in the name of God is going on? Where is her daughter?"

"Please get in. We're wasting time."

Trembling from head to foot, Britt climbed in. As soon as they were seated, the rotor began to turn. They hovered briefly, then rose at a steep angle and headed out over the water. The pilot looked over his shoulder. "We'll be at Newport Beach in a few minutes."

Arielle leaned forward and grabbed the FBI agent's shoulder. "Don't you get it? This is Megan's *mother*. What has happened to Megan?"

"I get it." The agent turned in his seat beside the pilot. "Dr. Thornton, your daughter disappeared very early this morning." He glanced at his watch. "Judging by information we've been able to gather, it occurred about sun-up, approximately fifteen hours ago."

"Fifteen hours! What have you been doing in the meantime? Why haven't I received even one message about this?"

"Honestly, ma'am, I am sorry. We first heard about the problem from someone named Oscar Plitman, whom I believe you alerted. He contacted the local police, and then, at their request, the Bureau. He suspects the person she is with of murder, and he has continued to advise us.

"At first, our information was sketchy. But it is clear that your daughter slipped out of the house before her grandmother was up, with the intention of meeting the suspect. Once we were apprised of the situation, we deactivated your phone and transferred your number to one of ours, which we are monitoring.

"Our first break came around two p.m., when the girl sent a couple of photos with text messages to you. She believed they were just out on the water for a lark."

Both women gasped. "Out on the water?"

"In a thirty-seven-foot sailboat. We traced the boat in her photos to one of the marinas. A witness saw her get on board just after sunrise, and another saw the boat leave shortly afterward. According to the office at the marina, the guy she's with has been doing some work for the owner. He was allowed to live on board as compensation. By the time we learned this, it was four o'clock, just three and a half hours ago.

"We did not hear from Megan again, but we tracked her phone. We got a fix on their location and sent a patrol boat out to make a positive identification. The suspect fired off a message. He identified himself as 'the unlucky number,' and warned that if we got close, Dr. Thornton would be sorry."

"I am certain of that. Is that the latest news?"

"Yes. So far as we know, Ma'am, your daughter is okay."

Britt closed her eyes. "Thank you," she whispered. "Thank you." She gripped Arielle's hand. "Where are they now?"

"Right now, they're just outside the jetty, holding pretty much in one spot. They appear to drift with the current a while, then motor back to their original position. We're staying back, but with binoculars, we can see both of them moving around on the deck."

"What's your plan?" Arielle asked.

"Our best chance is to send a dive team out to swarm the boat as soon as it gets dark. Right now, he'd see them. The water's absolutely clear, and he's patrolling back and forth."

Britt bit her lip. She had to think. To do that, she must keep a clear head. One thing was certain: It was too long a time to wait.

The helicopter descended in a slow, elliptical pattern toward the roof of a long, low building next to a row of docks with boats of all sizes tied up. It settled on a big white X.

In a few minutes, they were in an air-conditioned room full of agents and officers, all men. Britt sank into a chair at the end of the table where they all sat. Arielle pulled up a chair and squeezed in beside her.

To a man, they were in favor of sending a dive team. After sunset. They would overwhelm him.

Britt shook her head. "Not a good idea. I must go out there. Now."

The officer across the table glared at her. "We wait until dark."

"No. He will not wait. He's seen the patrol boat, so he's already suspicious, and darkness will only make him nervous."

All the men started talking at once.

She tried not to hyperventilate. "He has poor impulse control, and he—"

Their voices drowned her out.

Arielle climbed up and stood on her chair. "Stop!"

They gazed at her with their mouths open.

She got down but remained standing, her hands on her hips. "You all need to listen to Dr. Thornton. Every one of you. This is her area of expertise. And Megan is her daughter."

One of them stood, braced his hands on the table, and leaned in. "We know what we're doing. But we won't wait. We'll go with plan B."

"Which is?" Arielle asked.

"We'll create a diversion, a couple of party boats

with music and dancing. That will distract him and cover the dive team."

Britt got to her feet. "That is the dumbest thing I ever heard. You are seriously underestimating him. My daughter will be dead before you get anywhere near."

"It's our best option."

"It's a bad one."

A phone lying on the table rang. The man across from Britt reached out a big brown hand and touched the screen, accepting the call. A moment later, Thirteen's voice sang, "Doctor Britt, I love your little daughter. We are just as close as close can be." He cackled. "Bet you didn't expect to hear from me again, but I do so want to see you. Don't take too long. I'm not good at exercising patience, you know."

Britt reached for the phone.

The man ended the call. "Plan B. Let's move."

"Stop." Britt glared. "You don't know this guy. He's playing for keeps."

The phone rang again. This time, Thirteen said, "I saw that helicopter, Doctor Thornton. I know you're here. Put on a bikini, dear doctor, dear doctor. A teeny, tiny bikini. Nothing else. Then get in a small boat all by yourself. Motor away from the dock. When I see you coming, I will tell you what to do next." He hung up.

Britt said, "I'm going, and damn you all to hell if you interfere."

A text message showed up on the screen.

—*I may not be able to stop my very sharp knife from doing what it does best.*—

There was a photo of him with his arm around Megan, holding her tightly against his chest. Her eyes were wide, pleading.

Arielle started toward the door. "I'll get a bikini. You men need to find a boat she can drive with one hand." There was a moment of silence, while they all looked at each other. Finally, a couple of them nodded.

Half an hour later, Arielle helped her down into a twelve-foot pram with an outboard motor. "The force is with you, Britt," she said. Tears flooded her eyes. "Don't forget it." She hugged Britt hard and climbed back onto the dock.

Clad only in a bright red bikini, her cast no longer supported by the sling, Britt motored slowly away from the docks, then threaded her way between cruisers coming and going through Newport Bay. How was she going to do this? She had never shot a gun in her life. She hated guns. What if she fumbled getting the little pistol out of the makeshift holster the agents had fixed to the inside of the cast? What if she dropped it? She fought down a wave of nausea, tried to focus on breathing slowly and steadily. Okay, assuming she had it in her hand, would she actually be able to pull the trigger?

At last, she passed Balboa Island, turned right, and ran along beside the jetty until she reached open water. The evening breeze had whipped up a light chop, but the little pram handled it well. She sped up, eager to get this done. The sailboat, alone, gleaming white, loomed larger. The phone chimed, and when she picked it up, Thirteen said, "Slow down, please, dear Dr. T."

She cut the throttle, slowing to her previous speed.

"That's right," he crooned. "Now head this way nice and slow. Keep the phone on so I can talk to you."

Out in the ocean, with the occasional wave breaking over the bow, away from other boats, she felt vulnerable, alone. A police helicopter passed overhead, but that was no comfort. She could only hope that the police inflatables designated to come to her aid were as fast as they claimed they were. Ahead, on the deck of the sailboat, she could see only one figure, his. She bit her lip to keep from begging him to let her see Megan.

His voice came clearly through the phone, which she had laid on the seat beside her. "Stop when you are twenty feet away."

Britt gritted her teeth. She tried to sound as if merely announcing that she was going to the grocery store. "I'm on my way."

She wanted to bargain, to demand that he let Megan go. But this was all about power, and that would be a sign of weakness. Twenty feet away, she shifted to neutral. The little boat rocked gently. It drifted forward a bit, then stopped.

"Now stand up so I can see you," Thirteen said.

Carefully, she stood, got her balance, and lifted her good arm away from her body. Her broken arm hurt like the dickens, but she stood tall and straight, looked her tormenter in the eye, and prayed that he couldn't see the bulge on the inside of her cast.

He gave a long wolf whistle. "Nice suit."

"Prove to me that my daughter is with you."

"Sure, sure Doctor T. She's right there." He pointed to the stern, and Britt caught a glimpse of Megan, sitting on a seat beside the wheel, her mouth covered with duct tape, her hands twisted behind her back, her cheeks shining with tears. Then he stepped in front of her, hiding her from view.

"Turn all the way around, Brittany," he caroled as he twirled a finger in the air. "Nice and slow."

Carefully, she edged around in a circle. Then she sank back down onto the seat and put the motor in gear.

He smirked, pulled Megan to her feet, held her in front of him, and beckoned with his knife. As Britt brought the pram parallel to the stern, he crooned, "Nice and easy, Britt. I think I may call you Britt now, since we are going to be all cozy and intimate."

She cleated the little boat off to the swim-step and climbed on board. She held Megan's gaze for a moment, trying to reassure her. Megan's eyes glittered with fear. She shook her head back and forth and struggled against her captor.

"Quiet, little sis." He held the knife blade, slender and shining, against her throat. "I'd hate to ruin your cute little neck."

Megan's face blanched. Tears rolled down her cheeks, but she didn't move.

Thirteen grinned. "Step right on in, Brittie. Join the party. We're heading out to sea. The three of us. Take the helm, please. The engine's running. Let's go. Get us out of here."

Britt moved past him to the helm in the center of the cockpit. Holding Megan like a shield, he pivoted so that he stayed facing her. She put her hand on the wheel and peered at the gauges, as if to do as he said.

He lowered the knife and pointed it at the throttle. "Step on it."

She swung her cast. It hit his arm just above the wrist. The knife spun out of his hand, clattered to the deck, and skittered to the opposite side. Thirteen lunged for it.

Britt brought the cast down on the back of his neck. He sprawled flat.

The little pistol fit nicely in the palm of her hand. Hell, yes, she'd shoot him if she had to.

He scrambled up to all fours.

She pressed the barrel into the back of his neck. "Get back down. One wrong move and you're dead, creep."

Chapter Thirty-Seven

Chevalier

Jean-Luc stood in the cool, dimly lit cheese aging cellar, turning the large, heavy wheels of Gruyère and Emmental on the top shelf. Beside him, Jacqueline turned the small cheeses on one of the lower shelves. As they worked, they inspected each round to assure that they were smooth and firm—perfect, in fact. Normally, Jacqueline would be chattering about school, about the kittens in the barn, about whatever might be on her mind. But for the last few days, she had been quite silent. Her little face looked pensive. She sighed.

He looked down at her. "What is it *Ma Petite*? Are you having some problem at school?"

She turned another cheese. "No, Papa."

"Is there a boy who doesn't like you?"

She tipped her head up for a moment. Her wistful smile made his heart lurch. "No, Papa."

"Well, let me think, then." He put his head to the side, a finger on his moustache. "Perhaps you are angry with me. What have I done to make you unhappy?"

She shook her head. "Nothing, Papa." Her hands trembled as she reached for another cheese.

He took her hands in his and turned her to face him. "Now, then, I know it is something, and whatever is the problem, I will help you."

Her eyes filled with tears, and her chin quivered as she drew in a deep breath. "When am I going to die?"

Jean-Luc's eyebrows shot up. His eyes opened in amazement. "To die? *Ma Petite*! What kind of question is that? What makes you think such a thing?"

Her grip tightened. She stomped a foot. "Don't pretend, Papa. You can't fool me. Viane's *maman* said I would die before my birthday." Her face crumpled, and tears poured down. Her nose started to run.

He held both of her hands in one of his. He pulled a handkerchief out of his pocket and blotted the tears. "And you have been worrying about this all the time since that night. My poor child, didn't I tell you she cannot do such a thing?"

"All the girls at school say she can. They say she's an old-time medicine woman, and they have magical powers, and I am going to die, just like she said." She pulled in a shuddering breath and started to sob.

He hugged her to his chest. "You should have told me at once. I know exactly what to do. I know just the right thing. You must not worry for another minute. Not even another second." He rocked her gently back and forth until her sobs lessened.

He dropped a kiss on top of her head and handed her the handkerchief. With both hands on her shoulders, he held her away a little and peered down at her. "You will live to be very old, much older even than your *grand-père* and *grand-mère*. Nothing will harm you; I promise." He lifted her chin and waited until she looked into his eyes. "I know someone with more magical power than anyone. Come. We must go right now. Then you can show the girls at school that you have something much stronger than a fake medicine woman's curse."

Chapter Thirty-Eight

Chevalier, the following March

Jean-Luc heard the mistral begin. A gust slammed into the side of the house. Here in Provence, winter was over, but this wind would blow right into Jacqueline's room, bringing rain, debris, and icy fingers of cold from the frigid north. He opened her door, tiptoed past her bed, and closed the window, shutting out the tingly scent of ozone. As an afterthought, he pulled the curtains together, even though the caulking he had worked into the ancient wood frame left not even one crevice.

The old stone house was snug and safe. In the light streaming in from the hall, he could see her slender fingers clasped around the golden angel on the gold chain that she wore day and night. Nine months had passed since he gave it to her, and she had never taken it off. He pulled a blanket up over her shoulder and tiptoed back to the living room.

He added a log to the fire and closed the screen to contain the shimmering, dancing sparks. A glass of cognac in hand, he sank into his worn leather chair and propped his feet on the ottoman beside the hearth. He picked up his book but didn't read.

Viane's trial had progressed rapidly. Tomorrow, he would sit behind her in court and hear the judge read the verdict. It would be his last act as her husband.

The evidence that she poisoned him was irrefutable. He could live with that. But the charge that she murdered his parents sat like a lump of clay in the pit of his stomach all day, every day. He'd given the Gendarmerie permission to exhume and examine their remains. And, hoping to prove that she was innocent, paid a reputable attorney to defend her.

After listening to the arguments, it didn't matter that she refused to admit guilt. It didn't matter what the court decided. He knew. And Didier was right. It was past time to divorce her.

Jean-Luc put the book down and got to his feet. He strode across the room to the hallway, lifted a thick wool jacket from a peg near the door, shrugged into it, and went outside.

He spread his arms and leaned into the mistral, felt it blow around him and go on its way, cold and strong. He never complained about the wind. It took away everything old, stale, and decayed; always, when it finished, the world felt new again, fresh and vital.

Tomorrow the tempest would blow over him and all around him. He would grieve again for the death of his parents, and at their graveside, he would beg forgiveness. Then, pray God, he could forgive himself.

****

The mistral moaned through Chevalier's town square, and somewhere nearby, a loose shutter banged against the side of a building. In the dim light of early morning, Britt looked across the tiny bedroom at the other bed. How Arielle could sleep with all the noise, she had no idea.

She pushed aside the blankets and swung her feet

to the floor. Her toes found the soft plush of her slippers and she slid her feet into them. Shivering, she groped for her robe, found it lying at the bottom of the bed, and pulled it on. She snugged the belt around her waist, and then tiptoed into the cozy sitting area, closing the door behind her.

She switched on the lamp above the window, and a puddle of light shone down on the old wood table. Arielle had chosen to keep the furnishings Monique left, and whereas the apartment had seemed shabby at first, now it felt warm and welcoming.

As Britt's laptop came to life with a cheerful trill, she scooped coffee into the French press and heated some water. She clicked on the symbol for a video call, and in moments her mother's suntanned face appeared on the screen. She lounged by the pool in her backyard, wearing a big hat and a strapless black swimsuit. She lifted a short, fat tumbler with a pineapple spear sticking out of the top. "Cheers, darling." She leaned forward, cocked her head to one side, and frowned. "What's that awful noise?"

Britt laughed. "It's the famous mistral, Mom." The wind whistled through the gap between the warped wooden window frame and the stone sill, filling the apartment with the smell of rain. "It's blowing about fifty miles an hour. It's freezing cold, and everyone is cranky."

"It's a perfect evening over here, darling. I don't know why you won't come and live in Newport Beach."

Britt bit her lip. How many times did she have to have this conversation? "Mom, you know very well that I work in Seattle."

"I also know you could do your work from anywhere. Megan is loving it. School is going well, and she's made some good friends. It would be better for her to continue school here."

Britt sighed. During the three months of Rob's recently concluded trial, her only comfort had been that Megan was spending the year in California, shielded from the local news and gossip that swirled around him. More than that, the fear that she would also be deemed culpable and sent to prison had terrified and threatened to consume her. It would have been impossible to keep Megan from being swept up in all the tension and outright worries if she had been in Seattle.

Those three months were, hands down, the worst time of Britt's life. Frequently, she still jolted awake out of a deep sleep, sitting up in bed with her heart pounding. Then, when Rob's trial was over, almost immediately, in spite of depleted energy and exhausted emotions, she had returned to Chevalier to testify in Viane's trial.

She drew in a deep breath. "I know you'll miss her, Mom, and I can never thank you enough for taking care of her this year, but she has friends at home, too. And she can still spend summers with you. And you can come and visit anytime. Can I talk to her? What's she doing?"

"She's in detention with the school counselor, then has marching band practice."

"Detention? What's that about?"

"She and her best friend had a scuffle in the locker room today. Apparently, they both like the same boy." Her mother smiled. "I seem to recall a similar incident when you were her age."

Britt frowned. "It's not the same at all. I should be there."

"Now, dear, I raised you, and you turned out fine. I promise that I'm not taking this lightly."

"I do trust you." *But I haven't been much of a mother lately, and I hate that.*

Her mother took her sunglasses off, leaned toward the screen, and squinted. "What's wrong? You look nervous. You're through testifying, aren't you? Isn't this the day you hear whether that awful woman is convicted or not?"

"It is."

The last day she'd have to pretend she didn't know Jean-Luc Thibaudet was in the same room.

****

Jean-Luc stood in a back corner of the courtroom, waiting for the last minute to take his seat. His head snapped up, and his eyes fastened on Brittany Thornton as she walked in. She wore a black jacket, a black skirt, a pearl-gray blouse with an open throat. There was no color in her face, and she wore no jewelry. She looked straight ahead. Near the front, she slipped into a seat.

It pained him to see how thin she looked, her face especially. And the sparkle was gone from her eyes. During her husband's trial, he had taken to watching American news. He'd caught glimpses of her on the witness stand, and although he tried to stoke his anger against her, he found himself admiring her courage.

When she arrived in Chevalier to attend Viane's trial, she approached him, holding out her hand, and he turned his back. On the days when she testified, he stayed on the far side of the court.

From time to time, he could feel her gaze, and

always, when she came in and went out, his eyes followed her. Still, he could not bring himself to speak to her.

He walked down the aisle and sat behind Viane.

Chapter Thirty-Nine

The Midwest

Sitting at a card table in a bookstore in Minneapolis, Britt glanced at the line that had been straggling toward her for the last thirty minutes. Only a few more. Nearly done. And then what? Another hotel room. She loved connecting with people who wanted to read her book, but traveling to a different city every day, not so much. She gripped her pen, inscribed the purchaser's name, and signed. Smiled. Chatted. Thanked. Four more. Three more. The store lights dimmed. Only the area where the store held author readings remained illuminated. The events manager appeared, assured her that they would not lock her in, and waited to usher her out. Sign. Smile. Thank. Two more. One.

Professionally, Britt's capture of Thirteen had brought gratifying recognition, and her analysis of Oscar Plitman's research and the presentation of it in Beijing, which followed soon after, solidified her reputation as a psychologist.

But it was her failure—her failure to recognize Rob for what he was—that sold books and lectures and made her name a household word. She had written her book, *Secrets of the Very Married*, between days on the witness stand last winter, in the dark, sleepless nights.

Published before the notoriety of Rob's trial died down, it hit the bookshelves like a blizzard and generated more income in two months than she had earned in the previous five years.

Britt dropped her pen and her own copy of *Secrets* into her book bag and got to her feet. She thanked the events manager, and together they headed for the door. Near the exit, a man wearing slacks and a sport jacket stepped forward. "I happened to be in the neighborhood," he said.

Britt took in a quick breath. "Stan Gibson." Her hand fit nicely into his warm, firm palm, and he held it there. She smiled. "Are you following me again?"

"Don't worry, you're not in trouble, not this time." He smiled back. "I notice that you've made lemonade out of your lemons."

"So, you dropped by just to coin a cliché?"

"Clichés are not usually so pretty."

She met his open, friendly gaze and saw something more. He looked hopeful. Britt raised her eyebrows. "How does one happen to be in Minneapolis?"

"My niece's wedding. Big family gathering, you know. And I was due for a trip home. Would you like to join me for a walk?"

It was exactly what she wanted to do, and she hadn't known until he asked. "I would."

They strolled away from the store in the long evening light, in the warmth of early summer. They chatted as if old friends, talked of families, of weddings, of the flow of life from one generation to the next, and all the things that matter to us on this planet. They sat on a bench in a park, surrounded by blue pansies and purple coneflowers and pale pink geraniums. They watched the light fade from the sky, heard the city settle for the night, and he put his jacket over her shoulders when they stood to walk back to her hotel. They stopped at a wine bar to taste a flight of reds and walked some more, until after midnight.

Until it was time to decide. In the lobby of her hotel, Britt gazed for a long moment at the elevators. Stan took her hand in his. She turned to look at him.

He put his fingers on her mouth, gently. "I would like very much for you to invite me to your room. Very much." His steady brown eyes peered into hers. He tucked her hair behind her ear, lifted her face to his, and kissed her. His lips felt warm, soft, and inviting.

She started to lean into him, wanting more, wanting to feel safe and warm and cherished. But from far away, Jean-Luc pulled at her as the moon pulls at the tides.

He had looked right through her that day in March when Viane was convicted of poisoning him and killing his parents. Regardless, a current barely under the surface tugged, sometimes toward him, sometimes away. Come. Go. She could not go forward until she went back.

Stan cupped her face in his hands. "You know how to find me." He kissed her forehead, then turned and walked back across the lobby.

Chapter Forty

Chevalier

Édouard Chevalier's heart felt full, generous, content. "*Bonsoir*, Brittany, Arielle, Megan," he called. "It is a beautiful evening, *n'est-ce pas?*"

He carried his sleeping daughter in his arms. Monique strolled beside him, singing a soft lullaby. They had walked around the square several times, as was their habit, and now it was time to put the baby to bed. They stopped in front of Monique's grandparents' B&B. He kissed his child and handed her to Monique. They talked for another moment, and then Monique went inside. He turned toward the street leading to the bottom of the hill, his shadow ahead of him, stretched long in the waning sunlight.

He understood why Monique refused to get married. He'd been delighted when she told him she was pregnant with his child and that she had broken her engagement with Henri Lacoste. But she'd been adamant that the pregnancy was not a reason to accept his ring.

However, now that little Simone was seven months old, even though they lived separately, they had become a family. Édouard rarely stopped smiling.

****

When Arielle had mention she needed help in the

cheese shop for the last two weeks in August, Britt hadn't hesitated. And now, as she walked back from the restaurant after dinner with Megan and Arielle, she felt as if the old stone buildings surrounding the square, their edges softened by time, lace curtains fluttering in the windows, welcomed her back. It tickled her to see the same four old women sitting in the evening sun, side by side on the bench near the fountain. "*Bonsoir*," she said, as they passed by.

"*Soir, soir, soir, soir,*" each one murmured in turn.

Britt couldn't help smiling at how carefully Édouard cradled the baby and how happy both he and Monique looked. She waved and returned his greeting.

Arielle linked one arm with hers, the other with Megan's. "Everybody thinks they will get married soon." She grinned. "Want to guess when? I'm running a betting pool on the date."

By the time Britt opened her eyes the next morning, Arielle had already left to meet a tour group. She stretched, yawned, put some water on to boil, and measured coffee into the French press. It was market day. She meandered to the window, leaned her forehead against the already-warm glass, and stared down at the square.

Jean-Luc would be there. Soon he would set up his market stall and lay out his beautiful rounds of cheese, his sausages, his hams. Handsome, comfortable, full of life, he would be in his element.

Her heart, full of hope, beat faster. But she must not expect too much. It was entirely possible that he would refuse to speak to her. She must be prepared for that and not let it hurt her. Of course, he didn't have to know she was there. Maybe that would be best. If she stayed inside until he left—

"Mo-o-m." Megan flounced out of the bathroom, her hair tied up in a towel, her long suntanned legs sticking out of her favorite, and very short, shorts. "That kettle has been whistling forever already. Turn. It. Off. It's making me deaf." A tight black tank top hugged her torso, and proclaimed, in giant, glittering, gold letters across her well-developed fourteen-year-old breasts, *BITE ME.*

Britt pressed her lips together. She would not even think about the cute linen dress she'd bought for Megan in Paris. She might as well get used to the idea that it would spend the entire two weeks hanging in Arielle's closet.

Megan yanked the door of the refrigerator open, grabbed the orange juice, and banged it down on the counter.

Deep inside, something snapped. Britt sucked in a breath. "Look, you do not need to go on and on. I know you're unhappy about living in a condo when we go home, and I do so totally get that you think I'm a terrible person."

"Du-uuh." Megan rolled her eyes. "You helped send my dad to jail. And it's all anybody ever wants to talk about. My jailbird father and him having sex with Graciella."

"Honey, turn off your phone. You don't need to listen to all that."

"I do so. They're my friends."

"They will find other things to talk about soon. In the meantime, you have to face the fact that your dad went to prison because he committed a serious crime."

"You didn't need to tell about *her*."

"I did. She was part of it, and you don't lie in court."

"If you love somebody you do, but oh, no, not you. You stuck a knife in his back." Megan gave her that stony face, mouth shut in a grim little line, blue eyes steel-hard.

Britt so did not want to have this conversation again. She glared back. "I'm going outside. Dry your hair and come downstairs." She stomped down the old stone steps and out into the square. With a sigh, she sank into a chair at the café next door.

A little more than a year ago, she had been sitting at this same table and looked up to see Jean-Luc unloading his truck. The memory was as clear and sharp as if it had happened yesterday. He looked so handsome, so sure of himself, so comfortable in his own skin. And for the briefest moment, when his fingers touched hers, the windows of their souls opened to each other. But now his angry tirade, the words he'd flung at her in her hospital room, so bitter and full of pain, stood between them.

Megan bumped the table with her hip. "I'm here," she announced. "You said to come down, so I'm here."

Followed by her pouting, silent daughter, Britt wound her way down the hill, past worn stone steps, weathered shutters, and pots of red geraniums. At the bottom, just before the bridge, she stepped off the road, ducked her head under the trailing branches of the old willow, and emerged in the grassy meadow. This tiny green corner of the world, the gurgling stream, and the daisies bobbing in the breeze always soothed her soul.

They needed to talk, not only about Rob and his conviction for Medicare fraud, but about Thirteen.

After that day on the sailboat, Megan had refused to discuss what had happened, preferring to believe that it had been a lark, a prank meant only to scare Britt. In her mind, he was unjustly accused.

Britt slipped off her sandals and stepped into the water. "Come on. Let's get our feet wet." She stood in the middle, enjoying the coolness, the smoothness of the pebbles under her feet, and the strength of the current as it rushed around her knees.

Megan splashed across and plopped down on the grass. She sat cross-legged, scowling and tearing up handfuls of grass and tossing them into the water.

Britt resolved to say nothing. She had thought this vacation would ease Megan's transition from an entire year in California with her grandmother to the condo and school in Seattle. She had hoped they would both enjoy it. So far, "enjoy" wasn't exactly the right word.

Through the willow branches, she glimpsed Jean-Luc's red panel truck rolling over the bridge and reminded herself to keep breathing. The truck vanished from sight, but she heard it stop for a moment and then go on.

Jean-Luc's dark haired, brown-eyed daughter ducked under the willow and kicked off her sandals. She wore a white cotton dress that fell straight from her shoulders to her knees. "*Bonjour*, Madame Thornton. It is a surprise. I did not know you had come."

"Jacqueline, it is nice to see you, *bonjour.*"

The girl waded out, lifting her skirt to mid-thigh. "May I come and practice my English?"

"Certainly. But be careful. It's slippery out here in the middle."

"I know." She balanced there, studying the water.

"Papa did not tell me you are here."

"Perhaps he does not know."

Jacqueline shaded her eyes with a slender, suntanned hand and gazed up at Britt, her eyes questioning. "Papa knows everything."

"He was very angry with me the last time he spoke to me."

"Because you tricked Viane, and he found out how bad she is."

"It was a shock to him to learn that she poisoned your grandparents."

Jacqueline nodded. "To me also. But more to Papa." She turned, looked at Megan, and then waded toward her. "*Bonjour,* hello."

As if she hadn't heard, Megan got to her feet. She picked up a stone and skipped it across the stream. Jacqueline went and stood beside her. She stooped, selected a pebble, and threw it. It sank immediately. "May you show me how to jump it on the water?"

Megan picked up another. "Skip," she answered, her voice angry and condescending. "It's called skipping."

Britt wanted to smack her, but Jacqueline seemed not to care. She bounced up and down on her toes. "Skipping."

Megan's next stone skipped all the way to the far bank. "It's easy." Her frown began to fade.

"May you show me, please?"

"*Will* you show me."

Britt noted the anger seeping out of her daughter's voice.

"Will you show me, please?" Jacqueline repeated, her smile still bright. "And tell me the proper words?"

Megan bent and selected a couple of pebbles. "The best ones are flat, see?" She held them in her palm for inspection.

Britt offered a prayer of thanks. She turned her back to the girls and walked upstream, sat on a rock, put her feet in the water, and focused on her breathing, as she did in yoga class. A quarter hour passed. Time to get ready to open the cheese shop. As she started back, Megan laughed, something she hadn't done for days.

Jacqueline's voice carried clearly in the still morning air. "Viane's *maman* is a mystic, and she cast a spell on me."

"Cool. What kind of spell?"

"She cursed me so I would die."

"Wicked. How'd she do it?"

"She pointed her crooked, bony finger at me and chanted in an old-time dialect."

"But you aren't dead."

"No. Because Papa gave me an angel." Jacqueline pulled a long gold chain from under her dress and held it up to the light.

Megan reached for the necklace, but stopped, her hand outstretched. "May I touch it?"

"*Oui.* It is all right."

Megan turned the gleaming figure over in her hand, "It's beautiful." Slowly, she let it go.

Jacqueline tucked it back under her dress. She said, "He told me every time I am afraid, I should hold onto the angel."

"Do you do that?"

"Yes. *Certainement.* My papa is wise and good."

Megan's face closed like a poppy furling in on itself at the end of a sunny day. "Mine isn't." She turned back to the stream and grabbed a handful of stones.

Jacqueline gazed up at Britt, an anxious wrinkle on her smooth young brow.

Britt bit her lip.

The younger girl stood right beside Megan, elbows touching. Without speaking, she bent and scooped up a handful of pebbles and began dropping them one at a time into the water, just as Megan did.

Britt started back across, then turned in the middle and gazed at their lovely faces, their straight, slender bodies, and Jacqueline's long dark hair next to Megan's blonde. Her heart ached for both of them, for the lessons they grappled with now, and all the hard lessons yet ahead.

The girls stooped, gathered up more stones, and stood again, water dripping from their fists. One by one, they dropped them into the stream.

Finally, Megan spoke. "Can your papa get another angel?"

"*Certainement*. He can do anything."

"I have some money. Would he get one for me?"

Jacqueline gazed at Britt for a moment, her expression thoughtful. Then she turned back to Megan. "I don't think it works if you pay for it."

"Oh." A tone heavy with disappointment.

"I think he must give the angel to you."

Megan's eyebrows shot up. She stared at the other girl.

"And your angel must be especially for you. Come, we must ask him." As if she were suddenly in a hurry, she led the way across the stream, back to the road, and all the way up the hill.

When they reached the square, the vendors were not completely set up, but the earliest shoppers, women wearing summer dresses and carrying baskets, had begun to buy olives and tomatoes, cucumbers and carrots. Jacqueline took Megan's hand. "Madame Thornton, will Megan come with me to work with Papa today?"

"May," Megan said.

"May you come with me?"

"May I, Mom?"

Britt looked toward the center of the square. Jean-Luc's back was turned. "You said you would look after the baby for Monique while she works in the shop with me."

"I could take her in her carriage, couldn't I?"

"Let's go ask."

From the moment the cheese shop opened, Britt scarcely had time to breathe. She wrapped packets of cheese and slipped bottles of wine into market baskets. Monique made sandwiches and rang up sales on the ancient cash register.

A couple of hours passed before the girls came in, both flushed with morning heat. They carried the baby up the stairs to the apartment. When they came down, Monique's eyebrows shot up, and a grin of amusement crossed her face, but Britt was too busy to ask why.

At last, the stream of customers slowed. Édouard came in. Monique smiled at him. "Your *petite chou* is with Jacqueline and Megan. Do you want to find her?"

He returned with Simone balanced in the crook of his arm, her chubby fist clutching a handful of his shirt. He removed her sunhat, ruffled her wispy little curls, and kissed the top of her head.

Monique opened the cheese case and reached for a round of camembert. "Take a rest, Brittany. I will make Édouard's sandwich."

Britt hung her apron on the hook in the wine room, smoothed her hair back from her face, and walked out of the shop.

"Mo-o-m," Megan's voice called over the chatter of the vendors. She showed up a few steps away. "Mom, tomorrow may I go to the market at Gordes?"

Jacqueline hopped out from behind Megan. She pressed her hands together as if in prayer. "Please, Madame Thornton?"

Britt stared, wordless. Jacqueline had discarded her pretty dress for a pair of Megan's shorts and an old, worn, teenage witch tee shirt.

"Mom, we have a plan. She will speak only English, and I will speak only French."

Britt put her arm around her daughter. She inhaled the scent of sunshine and lavender as she dropped a kiss on her hair. Then a miracle occurred. Megan's arm slid around her waist, and she leaned against her—her little girl again. If only this moment would last forever.

When she looked up, from the middle of the square, Jean-Luc gazed at her, his arms folded on his chest. Closed. Clearly. His eyes looked as black as the stones in the stream. He was just now realizing that Jacqueline's new friend was her daughter. The offer to go to Gordes tomorrow would be withdrawn, and there would be no golden angel. And Megan would retreat into her surly self.

Britt opened her mouth to explain why they could not be friends.

But Jean-Luc was walking toward them, his arms

open. His gaze caught hers and held it. And then he stood in front of her. "Brittany," he said, in that funny way, Bree-tan-ee. His hands reached for hers and held them. "You have come at last. *Bienvenue*. Welcome."

Her lips trembled. Unable to speak, she lifted her face to his.

He kissed first one cheek, then the other, then the first again.

Tears blurred her vision.

"Children, go," he said with quiet authority. "Take care of my customers."

A word about the author...

I have studied writing in Paris and Seattle, and I write a monthly column for Pacific Yachting magazine. Murder Undetected is my second novel.

I am a physical therapist, a foodie, a fanatic about good chocolate, and a private pilot. I lived aboard an old wood motor yacht for seventeen years. In my dreams, I'm a famous author, a pianist of renown, an acceptable water-color artist, and a globe-trotting yogini.

http://roxannedunn.com